POODLE VERSUS THE ASSASSIN

COTTAGE COUNTRY COZY MYSTERIES - BOOK 1

ANNE SHILLOLO

D1529120

1

I was on my second glass of wine, and that was never a good thing.

Some people were wary of me because of my profession. Mind you, they usually acted friendly, at least to my face. This was because they knew that however drunk I might get, I, Zora Flynn, was going to wake up in the morning and still be the owner and publisher of the local newspaper, the Williamsport Whistle. Their fate was in my hands.

However, I was aware that others sneered. I suppose I deserved it. I mean, what woman of a mature age couldn't drink more than two glasses of wine without stumbling and talking nonsense? I'd been called a cheap date on more than one occasion. Although not recently.

I was close to my two-glass limit, but this event might put me over the edge. The Conservative Party riding association was having a convention to choose a candidate for the upcoming election. It was a waste of time, in my view, because they were a local dynasty. They could draw names from a hat, and their candidate would still be getting sworn in at Queen's Park a few days after the election.

It's not that I had a bias against the Conservatives. Well, maybe I did. But that would remain my little secret. Basically, all the parties annoyed me equally. And so my paper treated them all equally. I didn't say they liked it.

The Royal Canadian Legion was hosting the event, and I had certainly passed more pleasant times there in the past. It was a substantial building located on a leafy side street, with plenty of parking and friendly staff.

However, this evening's proceedings were grinding on. The event had opened with a bombastic, cliché-filled speech from Jasper Butler, the Conservative riding association president. I have to say, everyone other than me seemed to like it. He was interrupted many times with cheers and whistles. Jasper was a tall, portly man. He was dressed in a maroon plaid sports jacket and grey slacks, and the stage lights glinted off his cue-ball of a bald head.

He led us through the interminable stages of the candidate selection process. We'd had the candidates' speeches and a first ballot. It looked like there would be just one more vote. But they'd scheduled an intermission with live entertainment from a country band, whose banjo player was reportedly Jasper's brother. Regardless, they were a rocking good quartet. And the highlight of the event so far.

Even Jasper seemed to relax a bit, hanging his plaid jacket over the back of his chair and loosening his tie.

The room was filled with Williamsport movers and shakers. Everyone from business owners of all persuasions to Police Chief Arni Korhonen, to a crew of young voters. I knew they were all in their early 20s but, to me, they looked like they were up past their bedtimes.

As much fun as the people-watching was, I had to make my way to the restroom.

I stood up, sucked in my stomach, and tried to maintain a

steady gait as I walked across the dance floor, in front of the small stage, and over to the edge of the hall. The washrooms were located right at the side of the room, so at least I didn't have to navigate a set of stairs.

I pushed the door open and headed for the nearest stall, settling myself on the commode. Just as I was reaching for the roll of tissue, I heard the door open. A male voice let out a string of curses and my heart sank. I heard the telltale sound of a zipper and liquid hitting porcelain. I assumed a urinal.

How embarrassing. Obviously, I'd found relief in the men's room, instead of the ladies' facilities next door. As no one was in here laughing at me, I figured I hadn't been seen. I'd just have to wait until buddy was finished, and sneak back to the party.

In the meantime, I held my breath, and delicately picked up my feet in their ostrich skin booties. I rested them against the stall door just like we used to do when skipping class in high school. I examined the boots critically. I had taken to wearing tights and tunics in my advancing years. OK, I hadn't advanced much past 50, but why in the world any woman would wear anything less comfortable was beyond me. One thing about my wardrobe hadn't changed. Boots. I had the world's best collection. Well, probably not. But I bet no one in Muskoka could match me.

Were ostriches endangered, I wondered? There were some lines I would not cross. Although maybe I should think about the plight of any creatures donating their skins for boots before making the purchase. Whatever. I was positive the ostrich population was alive and well.

Suddenly I snapped out of my self-examination. Which usually didn't take much. I had heard the swoosh of the restroom door opening. My unseen companion's voice echoed slightly as he said sharply to the new arrival, "What are you doing here? I have nothing more to say to you."

Unbelievably, the next thing I heard was a shot. The music carried on, and I felt like my last minutes on earth would be accompanied by Folsom Prison Blues.

I heard the swoosh again, and I assumed the shooter had made his exit. I exhaled. No one was going to kill me. Not tonight, anyway.

But I knew I was not out of the woods yet. A pool of blood was flowing at a good rate under the door right towards me. I may be tough in an argument or as a boss. I'll admit it. But I had no stomach for gore. At the same time, it was now more important than ever that I slink out of the men's room as soon as possible.

I stood up, placing my feet on either side of the puddle, and straightened my clothing. I flipped open the lock and swung the door wide. To my genuine shock, Mayor Fred Phipps lay crumpled on his side, still leaking large quantities of his blood. I felt dizzy for more than one reason now.

Total embarrassment, as I was likely going to get caught in the men's restroom.

Serious nausea. All that blood. Some of which was seeping under my left boot.

And, OK, the wine I had on board.

I took a deep breath and analyzed my next move. I needed to step really far to my right, and then I could circle around Phipps to get to the door. It was going to be tricky. The stall door was hinged on the right side, so I couldn't hold onto the frame very well. But I was desperate. I took a huge step. And then disaster struck. It turned out I couldn't defy gravity. And my new ostrich skin boots were no match for a bathroom floor slick with blood. Not only did I fall, but Fred Phipps cushioned my landing.

The horror was unspeakable. Fred had been assassinated and here I was lying in the evidence. I swear I almost passed out. But adrenaline cleared my head pretty swiftly when the door

Poodle Versus The Assassin 5

swung open. I noticed the band was taking a break and that meant many gentlemen would be heading right this way.

Wouldn't you know it? Who was staring right down at me but a salesman from one of the car dealerships. He was a hearty man who coached minor hockey and had the voice of a foghorn.

He peeled his eyes off me and turned to the open door, yelling at the top of his lungs, "Arni, get over here. Zora's killed the mayor!"

2

S ure enough, Chief Arni Korhonen presented himself at the washroom door. My humiliation was complete. That man always brought to mind the phrase, 'If I were 10 years younger.'

With his Finnish heritage, Arni was tall, athletic-looking, and blonde, with calm hazel eyes. Everyone knew he was a runner, and I often passed him with a quick 'hello' when I was walking at night. He also had a reputation as a fish-whisperer. From what I'd heard, invitations to join his team in the various fishing derbies held on local lakes each season were coveted.

We had always gotten along very well. Nothing more than friends. But there were always days that I could use a friend. This would be one of them. Arni sighed, walked carefully over to me, and extended a strong, tanned hand. I grasped it gratefully and struggled to my feet, trying to step away from Mayor Phipps as quickly as I could.

I looked up at him and said, "I think you should lock the doors to the hall. Because I certainly didn't do this."

"Already done," he replied. "Zora, go next door and get

cleaned up. Then I'll see you outside. I need to talk to you, obviously."

I couldn't help wondering what this evening would have turned out like if I had gone into the ladies' room to start with. I might be bored but not bloodied. However, that ship had sailed. One way or the other I was entangled in the death of Mayor Fred Phipps.

Anyway, I exited the men's room, ignored everyone standing around the doorway, and went next door into the ladies'. The room was crowded with women wearing everything from jeans to power suits. The air was choking with the smell of hair product and perfumes of varying quality, and the decibel level was louder than when the band was playing. Until they spotted me. Then it was like the cone of silence had descended.

A dozen pairs of eyes were locked on mine. No one was showing any signs of vacating the bathroom, and I wanted privacy. I said, "Someone shot Mayor Phipps next door. Can you all just leave for a few minutes?" It never hurt to try the direct approach. "I don't know anything else."

Sure enough, they all filed out. After all, a quote from someone who had been on the scene was enough to get them headed back to share with their friends.

I took a long look in the mirror. The events of the previous ten minutes had sure sobered me up. A decade ago, I'd had long naturally blond hair and piercing blue eyes. I'd helped my hair along with some bottled dyes and potions and now it was a sleek white mane, with side-swept bangs over my right eye. I pulled it all forward and, with a shudder, examined it for traces of the mayor. All good.

It seemed like the only problem was the left sleeve of my tunic, which was fortunately made of solid black lycra. The bright geometric pattern on the rest of the loose shirt looked like normal

turquoise, coral, and black, with no unusual stains. I turned the
water on full blast and stuck my arm as far into the basin as I
could, telling my stomach to behave itself as I scrunched and
rinsed the fabric. The XLerator did a fine job of drying it.

I touched up my lipstick and then headed out into the
Legion hall.

Arni was seated at a large table off to one side. He looked
calm and professional in a pale blue Oxford shirt, button-down
collar open and sleeves rolled up. The convention delegates
were all seated, and I could see officers going from group to
group, with their notebooks and pens. On the one hand, I hoped
that they were going to end up with a definitive list of everyone
in attendance. On the other, that meant that the murderer was
in this room.

It was a shocking thought. As I looked around, I figured I
knew well over half by name. And still more by sight. The idea
that one of them would bring a gun to a public event and assas-
sinate the town's leader was hard to process. What in the world
had Fred Phipps done to bring this down on himself? He
seemed to be a kindly widower, ran a peaceful council table, and
was on his third term in office.

I headed towards Arni. In the seat facing him was Fred's
daughter, Jordan. It felt unkind to say she was a mess, but her
long dark brown hair was pushed back in tangles, her face was
pale and tear-stained and smeared with running mascara.

She looked like she had spilled a glass of wine down her
white lace t-shirt, and she was shaking her head in answer to
something Arni had said. Jordan was dressed casually in skinny
jeans and jacket, and wore trainers. Not quite a Muskoka tuxedo,
but close. For that, she would have needed a plaid work shirt,
and as this was June it would likely have been too hot. Although
others in the room had worn theirs.

As I got closer, I heard Arni say, "Again, I'm so sorry, Jordan. I can have an officer drive you home now. She'll also contact anyone you'd like to come over and stay with you."

Fred's daughter nodded and stood up, walking towards the door.

I took her place. Arni said, "Just start at the beginning, Zora."

"I was on my second glass of wine," I began.

Arni rolled his eyes.

I ignored him and continued, "I was headed to the restroom. By mistake..." I thought I saw another eye-roll but continued. "I entered the men's room instead of the ladies'." I carried on and told him the whole story. It didn't take long.

"OK," he replied. "So, you didn't know it was the Mayor when he came in?"

"No. He was swearing about somebody or something, but he didn't say enough for me to get the context or recognize his voice."

"What about the second person. Did they speak?"

"No. The mayor said something like, 'Get out of here. I have nothing more to say to you.' But the other person didn't speak. The next thing I heard was the gun."

"Can you be more specific? What did he sound like? Happy, surprised, angry, aggressive?"

That was easy. I said "He definitely sounded angry and belligerent. No humorous, joking, or friendly tones. More challenging. Sort of like 'who do you think you are.'"

Arni nodded and asked, "Did you hear anything? Did they clear their throat, did their shoes make a noise, did they have keys in their pockets?"

"I'm sorry," I said. "Absolutely no sound. And no smells either, if that's what's next."

"A work question. As the owner of the Whistle, you know a lot of the people in this room, and more local gossip than I do. I need to ask if you can think of anyone who might want to kill

Fred. Are you guys currently working on anything at all that might have a bearing on this killing?"

"No. That's all I've been thinking about. I haven't any idea who might be this angry at him. And we have nothing on the go. I'll meet with Brady and Olivia first thing in the morning and ask them the same thing."

Brady Kozak and Olivia Park were my two young reporters. I couldn't run the Whistle without them.

"I'll get in touch, too. I want to talk to them myself."

I nodded. The Williamsport weekly was hardly the Washington Post. If we found out anything, we'd share it.

"In the meantime, Zora, be careful. I gather you told the women in the bathroom that you didn't see anything. But we don't know if the killer got that message."

My blood ran cold. I'd thought the phrase was a metaphor until this moment. Of course. All the killer might hear was people joking about me being in the men's room at the time of the shooting. What if he thought I knew more than I did?

Arni interrupted my paranoid musings and said, "You're free to go.

3

I made my way home, walking slowly along the dark streets, in and out of the golden pools of light from streetlamps. The scent of new maple leaves on all the old trees was a sweet harbinger of summer. Warm light spilled from the windows of the houses, and I caught the occasional glimpse into people's lives: pictures on the walls, TV screens flickering, soft voices from shaded verandas. I felt like I was in a peaceful limbo. The events of the evening seemed like a distant nightmare. I allowed myself a few minutes of quiet enjoyment.

I lived right downtown. Talk about being in the center of the action, a perfect place for someone who published a newspaper in a small community. I prided myself on saying I never missed much. But I guess I had. The biggest crime in anyone's living memory, and I had no clue.

A few minutes later I was turning the corner onto Main Street. I had bought an old building a couple of decades ago. It had two traditional plate glass windows along the front, and behind those were two separate businesses. On one side was a café called Coyote Coffee that served tempting hot drinks and desserts starting at 7:00 in the morning. Talk about the perfect neighbors. The other side consisted of several small rooms and was my second home, the Williamsport Whistle newspaper office.

Upstairs was my apartment. Every year I vowed to rent it out and move somewhere bigger and fancier. Onto one of the beautiful leafy side streets, or maybe a lakefront property, or perhaps a new, modern condo. My place was the opposite of new and modern. I will admit it was quaint and scenic and suited me perfectly, but I'd had my share of problems over the years, from the rooftop to the pipes in the cellar.

My neighbors on either side were all commercial businesses, both at ground level and on the second floor. My home offered a lot of privacy, considering its location.

I let myself in through the door on the sidewalk, flipped the light on, and went upstairs, unlocking the door into my apartment. I got a big canine welcome. My dog was a beige whirlwind. He spun in circles, danced around on his hind legs, and clawed my knees. Is it any wonder I stopped wearing pantyhose about the same time as I got that animal?

His name was Rocco and he was a small poodle-bichon cross. His mother was a pretty 14-pound bichon frise. His father was an apricot poodle named Hank, who weighed in at 9 pounds. I never met him, but I bet he was a pistol.

Appearance-wise, Rocco was one hundred percent poodle. It was hard to believe, but all that personality was packed into 15 pounds of woolly beige dog. He was intelligent, intuitive, and a spectacular jumper. He measured 12 inches at the shoulder but it seemed like he could leap several times his own height. What a menace this made him!

People meeting him for the first time thought he was a puppy. He was skinny and hyper. But he'd been driving me nuts for 11 years already. During that time, I had coined the descriptor 'NSP' for my little pet. It was an obvious choice and stood for Nasty Small Poodle.

Roc always wore the same shiny royal-blue collar, studded with a row of gold, metal crowns. It was definitely a case of life imitating art. The longer he wore it, the more princely he became. And by princely, I meant demanding and vengeful.

Despite that, we made a good pair. I knew him so well that I thought I could sometimes hear him speak. But that was OK because usually, I agreed with his opinions. We both had the same snarky sense of humor. Unfortunately, he also sometimes turned his critical eye on me.

He was in fine form tonight. In the middle of his welcome-home routine, he suddenly backed away. *"Great Merciful Poodles! Where have you been? You smell... amazing!"* He lunged forward and began licking my ostrich-skin boots. And I don't think he was after the dead ostrich. More like dead mayor.

"Get away. That's disgusting," I muttered, sitting down and pulling the boots off. I set them in the kitchen sink. They could stay there until I figured out a way to clean and sanitize them. Preferably before I had to make my next meal.

I took a quick look around and everything seemed in one piece. I grabbed the leash, slipped into some flip-flops, and said, "Hey, Roc, time for a walk."

After the poodle had taken care of business, we went straight back upstairs. He was a creature of habit. He ran to his dog bed, which was parked beside mine, and barked at me to give him a biscuit. I knew he really wanted me to turn in as well, but I was much too wide awake for that.

I hopped in the shower, put on some striped flannel pajama pants and a camisole, and then decided to treat myself to a homemade latte. Normally, I thought it was way too much trouble when my pals downstairs could serve me in style, but I felt like I needed the activity of making espresso and steaming milk.

Once the foamy treat was poured, I bundled up in a fleece robe, turned the lights out and went to sit in the front window. I had a comfy, blue brocade wing chair and small, Victorian tea table positioned to give me great light for reading or to look out over Main Street.

I was well aware that none of my furniture matched, but each piece was a favorite.

I thought about the events of the night. As much as I had Fred Phipps pegged as a homespun, affable, upstanding mayor, he was obviously in the middle of something. What was the opposite of friendly, open, and law-abiding? Mean, sneaky, and criminal.

It was a pretty short list of things that usually caused people to kill one another, and somehow Fred had checked the wrong box.

My thought process was interrupted by the doorbell, followed immediately by Rocco losing his mind. He flew like a bullet to the door and flung himself at it, barking like a maniac. Honestly, it was a good job I had no neighbors. I opened the second-floor door and looked down at the street. My best friend, Marley, was unmistakable in her lime green running jacket. Roc sprinted down the stairs to attack her. He never used all four legs. Only three ever touched the treads as he descended.

I followed him at a sedate pace using both feet, and let her in. Of course, she ignored me, kneeling down and cooing, "Roc, Roc, Rocco. Big tough boy, come here." Marley scratched him behind the ears and ruffled up all his fur, and we all trooped upstairs.

I put the kettle on, and we settled down to drink tea. At this rate I was going to be up all night. Latte plus tea. I should know better.

Before the drinks were even poured, Marley started, "So. Fred Phipps. Tell me everything." We both laughed until we cried, not at poor Fred, but at my predicament. I played up the comical aspects of my visit to the men's room. But that was mostly to keep my fear at bay.

"Marley, I cannot think of a single person who would want Fred dead. Do you have any ideas?"

She shook her head. "He seemed to get along with everyone. In fact, I'd have to say, that had become his brand."

"What about his personal life?"

"Again, hard to come up with anything. He was such a well-known public figure, but I know virtually nothing else about him. His wife died a few years ago, and his daughter Jordan often attended events with him. But not as much lately. She's seeing Tyler Aston, the doctor's son. Last I heard, he was taking law at York."

"Well, I hope they solve this murder soon," I said quietly. "All kidding aside, even Arni mentioned it. Everyone knows I was in the bathroom, right?"

"For sure. Five separate people stopped me on my run to tell me."

"Well, I just want to spread the news that I have no idea who it was."

Marley paused. "Well, OK, then. I'll get busy."

I felt in safe hands.

Marley was very well-qualified. She had a main street business and networked constantly. She was tall, still had a figure like a model, and wore her hair long, wavy, and various streaked shades of blond. She had been divorced for many years, her ex lived a nice distance away and her one child was making his fortune out West.

That left her plenty of free time for sports teams, book club, music lessons, volunteering, and online kibitzing. If there were additional ways to network, Marley had not yet found them. She put me to shame. And I was in the communications business.

4

Rocco was lying in his office bed in a pool of sunlight, and my two young reporters sat across the meeting room table from me. Brady put his cup of coffee down, a rare occurrence. Olivia's jaw had dropped, and she recovered herself and closed her mouth.

I had just once again related the events of the night before, and I profoundly hoped it was for the last time.

Brady said, "Well. I had heard on the radio, and online, but I didn't quite understand your role, Zora."

"Same," said Olivia faintly. "You actually fell on him?"

I didn't deign to answer her. "Arni Korhonen will want to speak to you both."

They looked at each other, and Olivia asked, "Why? How could we possibly know anything? We weren't even there."

I replied, "I think he knew right away he was going to need outside information. There were apparently no witnesses. No one saw who exited the men's room before they found me. Everyone has been singing Fred's praises. There must have been 200 people at the Legion for this event. No one has a clue why someone would kill Fred, and in such a…"

"Violent?"

"Scary?"

"Yes. I mean guns. In town," I said. I agreed with them. We weren't talking about hunting or even poaching here. Or target practice in a sandpit. Welcoming in the new year. Sighting rifles before hunting season. Scaring off bears. Whatever. This was a different situation altogether.

They nodded at me.

I continued, "I want to decide on a course of action immediately. Obviously, we want to help the police if we can. But we also want to provide detailed news stories to our readers. Next week's paper won't be out until Wednesday, but I think we can do a pretty good job on a daily basis on the website."

Brady Kozak was not only a decent reporter and photographer, he was a whiz with technology. He had singlehandedly brought our boring website into the 21st century with a redesign and frequent updates. Usually, we would all meet first thing in the morning and decide what we would be using as daily news, and Brady would try to have it live by noon.

He said, "For today, we need your story, as the person closest to the event."

Olivia shuddered.

"Of course. You can write it up based on what I just told you. I also want a large headline stating, 'Zora Flynn saw and heard nothing.' You can change the wording a bit if you want, but that's the essential message. I don't want some crazy assassin looking for me next. Besides, it's true."

I continued, "Olivia, can you please get a statement from the police? Maybe tomorrow we can go with comments from the family and the rest of the councilors. Also, at some point, we have to do an update on the Conservatives' candidate selection process. Even if it's just to say the meeting will resume some other day and time. You can interview the riding association president, get the results of the first ballot, and so forth."

They both nodded again, and shoved their chairs back, ready to get to work.

"Not so fast," I said. "We're just getting started. This case is going to be hard to solve."

Olivia Park was a local girl, in her early twenties, just like Brady. She was presently sporting dyed red hair cut in a shoulder-length bob with bangs, which totally altered the Korean features her parents had given her. She reached up to straighten her hairband and said, "I agree. Mayor Phipps was a really nice guy."

"Yes. And those are the comments and tributes we are going to publish online today and tomorrow. But I want to leave you with an assignment. You've both been on the job here for over a year, right?"

More nods.

"Also, Olivia, you have a lot of local knowledge from growing up in Williamsport. You hang out with your parents and hear their opinions. You might have insights from your friends. You probably worked in a variety of places as a student. Later today, I want to meet again. At that time, I want a long list of every single person - other than the mayor - who has ever been suspected of anything from parking in a handicapped spot to stealing money. A very long list."

"Wow. I love it," said Brady. "Then we can look for connections back to the mayor."

Olivia added, "This is going to be fun. I was never a 'mean girl' in school and part of me is looking forward to acting out that fantasy. Do the things we list have to be true?"

"Of course not," I said. "And that's why it won't be necessary to share every last thing with Chief Korhonen. Facts, yes, scurrilous gossip, nope. OK, get busy."

Olivia began to push her chair back, and then yelled, "Ow."

Brady had obviously given her a kick in the ankle. He looked at her and then inclined his head towards me. "You better tell her," he said.

Olivia looked like a deer in the headlights. A moment passed. Then she sighed, covered her face with her hands, and said, "Fred and I were. Seeing each other." Then silent tears began pouring down her face.

From my left, I heard, *"Great Merciful Poodles."* I couldn't have said it better myself. I was astounded.

"You were sleeping with the mayor?" I asked incredulously.

"No," she said in a shocked tone, looking up at me. "My father would k..." More tears flowed. I could well imagine that Richard Park would get in line to shoot Fred Phipps if he thought the man had seduced his daughter. Richard was the quiet, strait-laced pharmacist in the downtown drugstore I patronized.

Hmm. My list of suspects had just got its first entry.

"Fine, fine. So, you weren't intimate. Olivia, the man was twice your age. Maybe more." I told myself to calm down and took a different approach. "Can you describe your relationship with Fred?"

She took a deep breath and began. It all came out in one stream of consciousness statement. "We went on dates. Fred made me feel really special. We went to lots of beautiful places in Toronto. He'd tell me to dress up and then we'd drive down for dinner or to go to a concert. Once," her voice caught, "Once we even flew down on Porter Airlines. It was so romantic."

The stream of tears intensified. "The last time I saw him, he gave me tickets for our next big night." She shifted her eyes away from me.

I paused for a second, and then the light dawned. "He got tickets to see Drake?"

She nodded, afraid to meet my eyes. I was well-known as a zealous Drake fan and had made a huge deal out of my disappointment at not scoring tickets to the upcoming concert. All my friends mocked me. In fact, I couldn't win. People my own age thought I'd lost my mind. Young people thought I was some kind of freak. I just liked the music.

And now Olivia would be going. It was so unfair. However, I set aside my bitterness and looked back at the pair of them. "Thank you for telling me. Are you OK to get to work now?"

Olivia wiped her eyes and nodded, "Yes. For sure. I want to know who did this more than anything."

"One last thing," I said. "I'll be blunt. I'm making a list, and you're going to be helping me with it later. But for now..."

I stood at the whiteboard and wrote my name, adding '- washroom of Legion.'

I cast a stern eye over at them as I then listed Brady, followed by Olivia. "Where were you both about 9:15 last night?"

Brady looked down, and then out the window. I was surprised. He seemed to live a pretty quiet life. But maybe I was in for another surprise. And it was, but a pleasant one.

He replied in an undertone, "At the gym."

I had never thought anything of the fact that Brady was carrying a few extra pounds on his stocky frame. He always looked great in his jeans and a varied wardrobe of Hawaiian shirts. I didn't make any comment, just wrote down his whereabouts and said, "Thanks. And you, Olivia?"

"I was home watching TV with my parents."

"Really?" I said.

"Yes," she finally smiled. "My dad is addicted to those reality shows where they send huge tow trucks to drag people out of horrific accidents. Then my mom and I got our way and we all watched a movie."

Neither of the reporters looked too offended at my interrogation. Soon after, they both left to get some work done, and I sat back with my first latte of the day. Our meeting room was at the back of the building and had a large casement window with a view of a pocket-sized yard and trees.

This room, along with the rest of the office, had originally been cloaked in cheap brown paneling. It was so depressing, I started tearing it down myself after two days. In short order, I'd hired someone and had the place drywalled and painted white, with dark wood trim in the usual places.

"Roc," I said, "We have work to do. Time for you to guard."

There was no response.

I popped him back upstairs with a biscuit and headed out.

5

Olivia's story, while shocking in and of itself, had got me thinking about something that had been bothering me about last night. Other than the whole debacle in the men's room, of course.

Fred Phipps had undergone a change in the last few months. Gradual changes, none of them noticeable on their own, but when you added them all up? Maybe it was a clue.

What had been a niggling observation was now something I wanted to think about. The reason I had never in a million years identified Fred as the man who entered the bathroom was the cursing. I had never seen Fred angry, let alone heard him swearing about anything. He was always calm and genial.

Now this morning, I'd learned that he'd been dating Olivia. She was definitely beautiful, and I could understand why any man would be attracted to her, but this May-December romance also seemed out of character for Fred.

Then I thought about his appearance. There had been changes there as well. I was a dedicated, maybe compulsive, walker. I liked nothing better than to stroll around town at night or early in the morning. Nearly every evening, Rocco and I went out about 10:00 p.m., and nearly every morning we made it at least around the block at 6:30.

Now that I concentrated, I knew it was only in the past six months that I had regularly seen Fred Phipps. Maybe long walks were a new routine for him? We never stopped to chat, but always said hello, or made a comment about the weather. That was usually good for a few seconds' exchange.

And over that six-month period, Fred had slimmed down. He'd also updated his wardrobe with understated but quality clothing, name brands, and a sportier look. The last time I'd seen him, he'd been wearing a really nice pair of jeans, a fitted black light wool sweater under a thin black vest and high-end black trainers.

To tell the truth, in the months before his death, the mayor had been looking pretty good. He had short sandy hair, graying at the temples, and warmer blue eyes than mine. Anyone would call him attractive. Not a tall man, his diet, exercise, and new wardrobe had given him a whole new look that suited him.

I had a terrible thought. What if he'd been diagnosed with a terminal illness? That would explain all the changes. What if he had a brain tumor? I knew my imagination was getting the better of me, but I'd had very little sleep. I decided to check in with Mr. Park at the pharmacy and see if I could do some snooping on my own before meeting the reporters at noon.

I put on my jacket. It was a gorgeous June morning, but still chilly. The sun was only shining on the west side of the street, and it was still cool on the east side where I was walking. The downtown looked picturesque and welcoming, quaint signs and picture windows gleaming in the morning light. It was just past ten o'clock, and all the stores were now open.

The wide street was lined with solid, two-story brick buildings. Our town had a population of about 20,000. It appealed to those of us who lived here as well as to the hordes of visitors that joined us in all four seasons.

From winter skiing to fall-color tours, spring festivals to summer cottagers, Williamsport was usually lively. Several large resorts, some luxurious and some rustic, were located nearby. And any town situated on a river, connecting to three lakes, would be a magnet for tourists. Thank goodness. Many services and businesses depended on them.

I entered the pharmacy and was happy to see that it was mostly empty of both staff and customers. I knew that was selfish of me, but I didn't think I would be here long. I headed to the back counter and caught Mr. Park's eye.

"Good morning, Zora," he said with a smile.

"Hi, Richard," I replied.

"I heard you had quite the adventure last night. Although I shouldn't even joke about it. Poor Fred," he said, shaking his head.

This was going to be easier than I thought. He had left me an easy opening to continue talking about the death of the mayor. I was also sort of happy that a) he didn't look guilty, which meant b) Olivia's secret love life was safe.

"Yes, it's not an experience I ever want to repeat." That was definitely true. "Richard, I haven't been able to stop thinking about Fred Phipps. He just seemed like the last person to come to a violent end."

"I couldn't agree more. A really nice guy, even if he was a politician."

"Did it seem to you that Fred had changed lately?" I asked.

The pharmacist reflected, "Now that you mention it. Maybe."

I decided to take my chance. "A lot of changes," I emphasized. "I can't help wondering if he was having some health problems."

Richard shot me a critical look and then softened his gaze.

"If I had to guess, I'd say probably the opposite. I think he was on some kind of health kick."

"I hope you're right," I said with a smile. I decided it would be a good idea to make a purchase while I was there. I think people assumed I was just naturally nosy, which was pretty accurate. But I didn't want it to seem as though I was exploiting them, day in and day out. I picked up some antihistamines off a sale rack, added a bottle of vitamins, and took them to the cash.

On my way back to the office, I stopped in at Marley's accounting business. She occupied a roomy storefront with a discreet gold-lettered sign on the window facing the street. It read *Marley Frey, CPA. Accounting and Business Services*. I said good morning to the receptionist, walked back to her spacious office, and sat myself down in her guest chair.

"Hi, Zora. How are you?" she asked with an expression of concern. She pushed her reading glasses up on her head, sweeping back her long, streaked honey-colored hair.

"I'm OK, thanks." I then regaled her with my theory about Fred Phipps and his recent transformation.

"A brain tumor? No way. People would know. He would have been to a doctor, a specialist, had imaging done. Someone would have said something. No way. If you ask me?"

"What? Yes, I'm asking you."

"Well, from what you describe, I'd say he was in love."

"Hmm," I responded noncommittally.

She continued, "It's obvious. I know that's how a crush affects me. Diet, more trips to the gym, new clothes. Fred had found someone."

The mayor's wife had passed away a long time ago. A very sad loss from cancer. Fred had taken it hard and had been single ever since.

I sighed. "I guess you're right. Fred must have been in love. Although I haven't heard anything about that either," I lied.

"That's a nice outfit, by the way. I love the lace effect." I was wearing denim-style tights and a light white tunic made of fake lace. Plus a denim jacket and my favorite cowboy boots.

"Thanks, Marley," I replied, and then stopped short, gazing into the distance over her shoulder.

"What," she said. "Are you OK?"

I snapped back to reality. "Perfectly fine. Listen. At the Legion last night, I saw Jordan Phipps, Fred's daughter, right after he was killed. She was the first person Arni interviewed, and then of course he sent her home. She also had a white lace top on. Although it was a crop-top," I said, curling my lip. Probably my least favorite fashion look ever since Madonna and Flashdance had popularized it and so many others had committed the travesty of wearing it. "Anyway, the front of her shirt was all stained. I assumed she had spilled her red wine in shock, and then tried to wipe it up."

"Ooh, I see where you're going with this," breathed Marley. "What if it wasn't wine?"

"Exactly," I said. "Of course, I assumed that the assassin was male. I mean what are the odds of two women being in the men's room at the same time? But I didn't see or hear a thing. It could have been ET or Elvis for all I know. It could certainly have been Jordan."

Marley hesitated. "Yes. I can see your point. But that's pretty cold, don't you think? First of all, handguns are illegal. So, she'd have to have somehow found a weapon, and been so full of hatred that she'd gun down her own father. I'm just not sure."

I nodded. "Good point."

But privately, I thought, that girl was remaining on my list.

6

I rushed back to the office and paused to talk to our rockstar production manager, Barbara Stevens.

I was always trying to streamline our operation. I knew we needed some of the trappings of the traditional print media, but when every second 14-year-old was broadcasting on YouTube for free, we had to trim things. The sales staff worked remotely, and Barbara more or less did everything from answering the phone to laying out the paper every Tuesday afternoon. Marley did all the business stuff.

I knew the office itself was a luxury, and we could all just work from home, but we needed a place to meet. My college years were a distant memory and I didn't want the reporters or interview subjects traipsing in and out of my apartment like it was a dorm room.

Barbara also had tremendous entertainment value, some of it intentional. She was in her late 20s but loved everything about the 1940s and 50s. It was as if when her parents gave her an old-fashioned name, they'd also channeled the culture of that era.

It was always fun to see her wardrobe choices from day to

day, not to mention the variety of bouffant hairstyles that could transform her dark-chocolate colored hair.

I managed to slide into my chair in the meeting room just in time. Brady and Olivia hurried in right behind me and sat down. We were all fortified with beverages from next door. I was starving but I thought I'd better hold out until the meeting was over so Brady could get started updating the website.

We all opened up our laptops and clicked into the Shared Documents area.

Brady said, "The stories for the site are ready. Let us know what you think."

I skimmed over the text and was very pleased with what the pair of them had come up with. I'd worked very hard with these two reporters, as I really thought they both had the right skills and attitude. But the main hurdle had been to get them to understand the difference between news and features. In this day and age, we needed many fast, succinct news stories for the website.

At the same time, they were both so creative. When I had hired them, they'd offered to update the website and get the Whistle onto social media. Olivia had set up an Instagram account for the paper and there the reporters were allowed to write other kinds of material. We'd had a long chat about libel and slander laws, and professional behavior. And the fact that it was going to be a business account.

But neither one of them really had the soul of a muckraker and, so far, the Instagram account had not only been successful but a popular hit with our readers.

I looked up from the screen, and said, "These stories are perfect. Excellent work. Brady, you can go ahead." He started clicking, cutting, and pasting.

I was proud of them. Here we were, the day after a truly calamitous event, and the website was being updated right on schedule. Brady also had some program running that posted the headlines as links on our Facebook feed. I sure had learned a lot about how to keep a publishing business afloat in the last little while. Thankfully, so far it was working.

I gestured to the whiteboard. "I want to get going on our list of possible suspects. Oh, did I say that out loud? I meant to say our list of 'Story Ideas.' Olivia, I see from the news stories that the chief didn't really give you anything."

She shook her head. "No, and I didn't expect him to. It was a very basic statement. They're working on the case, all possible resources, that sort of thing."

I looked over at them, with a hopeful gaze. "Anything good?"

Olivia said, "Yes!"

Brady hesitated.

"What?" I asked.

He replied, "I'm just not sure. Maybe it's from living in the city during the past few years, but these ideas seem sort of lame. Not worth killing over."

"Fair enough," I said, "But let's have a look at what you've got." I stood up, walked over to the whiteboard, and erased our three names. I grabbed a marker and popped off the cap.

Olivia started us out. "I was trying to come up with things I heard that sounded like corruption or undue influence. Some sort of connection to town hall."

I nodded encouragingly.

"Number 1. Last fall, Councilor Rigg's son, Sonny... Wait, I know that nickname sounds ridiculous. Anyway, he was caught driving over the limit, but when his drunk driving case came to court, it was dismissed. The officer didn't show up to testify. Now, if Mayor Phipps thought Councilor Rigg had done something to make this happen, which everyone thinks she did, by the way, it could have caused conflict between them. If the councilor thinks more of Sonny than she does of the mayor, she would never back down."

"Excellent!" I crowed. "This is exactly what I meant. Brady?"

"OK, Number 2. The mayor himself. His next-door neighbor is this old codger named Ollie Hanson."

"Oh, yes. I haven't thought of him in years," I interrupted. "He had a reputation for not really observing the hunting season dates. And, supposedly he catches a Canada Goose every year, pens it up in the bush behind his house, and fattens it up for winter."

Brady continued, "Yeah. That makes sense. Geez, I cannot believe I said that. My friends in the city would never let me live it down if this story becomes my claim to fame. Anyway, the mayor's pet was a big old Shepherd cross."

Olivia looked stricken, and her eyes filled. "He's a good dog. Fred named him Harper, after the prime minister."

This stopped me short. "One second. Here's one other thing I never thought of. I wonder what Fred was doing there last night anyway? I'm pretty sure he wasn't a Conservative."

Olivia smiled and said, "You're right. He said he named the dog Harper because the dog was full of, you know."

I had to laugh.

Brady said, "I'm sure it was the same reason you were there. It was a big event. It was important. It was public. Lots of people attended who weren't party members. Fred Phipps was a local dignitary. Anyway, back to the dog. Harper is allegedly always wandering next door, leaving a load on the neighbor's lawn. And, supposedly, Hanson said if he saw him one more time, he'd shoot him. He also told anyone who would listen that the bylaw officer was being paid off to not charge the mayor for his dog running at large."

I nodded enthusiastically and added Ollie Hanson to the whiteboard.

Olivia said, "When this is all over, I think we should do a story on that bylaw officer, especially as he is also the building inspector. I have two more related rumors. On Compass Lake, a seasonal resident finished their boathouse. It's about twice the size that's allowed in the zoning bylaw, and I heard it has a guest room on the second floor. The same person told me that two people have built garages out Maple Hill Road without any permits at all."

"Any names?"

"No. I can check further this afternoon."

"Well, these are good ideas." I added the points to our list. "In the old days, there were rumors that the building inspector would follow the lumber yard delivery truck to make sure that people buying materials had permits. Now, there was something that almost led to bloodshed."

Brady looked puzzled, and said, "But, I don't think these problems have anything to do with the mayor."

I let Olivia answer. She said, "I agree. But what if the whole system is corrupt, and some builders and contractors are being cranked for fees and watched constantly? Unexpected visits from the Ministry of Labor, Workplace Safety and Insurance Board, Standards and Safety, the fire department? While other people get to go ahead and build whatever they want."

He brightened up and replied, "I see your point. Plus, there could be other larger projects that we don't even know about. It sure seems like a system that's ripe for someone to try to influence."

I heard the outer door to our office open, as we had attached a string of bear-bells to it. You were supposed to wear them while hiking to warn all the wild animals that you weren't trying to sneak up on them. But they worked the same way on our front door. I remembered that Arni Korhonen was due for a visit.

"Quick," I hissed. "Take a picture of the whiteboard for me, please."

They both had their phones in action in a split second, and I erased the surface just as Arni called, "Anyone home?"

"Back here," I answered.

He entered the meeting room and sat down at the table. "Any news?" I asked, pretending that Olivia hadn't just spoken to him within the last hour.

He shook his head politely. "The weapon is going to be a stumbling block for sure. I mean who walks around with a handgun, anyway? At least that's one thing we don't usually have to worry about here. I'm calling the Ontario Provincial Police for help on that."

He pulled out a notebook. "The other officers are still out interviewing people who were at the Legion last night. They got a good list of names before we let everyone go home. But I have to say we're no further ahead. Please don't quote me. I've been up all night."

He added, "I'm well aware that you'll be looking for ideas yourselves. I warned you last night, and I'll say it again. This is something you should leave to us. Now, on the off-chance you've been comparing notes already, what have you got? Anything?"

I looked right at him and said, "Yes, we're curious of course. But with Fred being basically a really nice guy, none of us can think of a single person who would want to kill him."

And that was the truth.

7

W hat a day. I was so happy to climb the stairs up to my home sweet home.

I walked into the usual chaos. That nasty dog had tossed all the throw pillows off the furniture and was lounging in the corner of the sofa in the late afternoon sun. I yelled, "Off," and of course got the usual reply. He didn't even raise his head. Just swiveled his big, black eyes in my direction and said, *"Check the collar."* That was Rocco's response to most commands. Royal blue collar with crowns? He knew who ruled the roost. The Prince.

As I approached, he knew I meant business. Not that I'd ever hit him. For one thing, I wasn't fast enough to catch him. But if I raised my voice and waved my arms a bit, he'd obey me. He certainly understood English as well as most kindergarten children. He stood up, gave a languorous stretch, and hopped down.

I got a glass of iced tea and took over the sofa myself, replacing the pillows and settling myself down. After half an hour of total silence and relaxation, I heaved a sigh and got up. Time to get a load of laundry done and walk Roc. Then dinner.

I was just gathering up clothes and some linens when my

phone rang. My heart leaped. There was one call I was hoping for and I saw from the screen that this was it. Darius Bell. I shouldn't have been surprised at Olivia's subterfuge with the mayor. I'd been hiding my relationship with Darius for a couple of years now.

"Hi," I said cheerfully.

"Hi, Zora, what's new?" Darius responded in his sexy, low voice.

"You wouldn't believe it if I told you. But I will," I replied. "Are you coming up this weekend?"

Darius was at the top of the game in what he called 'fintech,' the latest buzzword that referred to integrating technology to support the financial sector. He talked a lot about the global economy and, logically enough, traveled all the time. My own integration with the financial sector consisted of monitoring my line of credit and Visa card balances so that Marley wouldn't yell at me for abusing them. Darius found this hilarious.

Ironically, we'd met at a free concert at Riverside Park the summer before last. We chatted for a while about music, and I even confessed my long-time devotion to Drake. Although I told him I liked all kinds of music. Our relationship was almost over before it began when he had said the same thing, adding, "Except bagpipes." But we had agreed to disagree. After the performance, we had gone for dinner at one of the downtown bistros and fortunately I had restricted myself to one glass of wine.

The next time I was in Toronto, I'd invited him to join me for coffee and one thing had led to another. And by that, I meant dinner. We ended up talking for hours and then walking along the lakeshore under the stars for a long time.

He confided in me that he was burned out from the media spotlight on his business and personal life. He admitted, "I can't deny I've benefited. All my ventures over the years have been successful." He shrugged. "I don't even think of the money anymore. I just want to work on things that interest me. With finance, I want to focus on apps that give consumers more independence. That's the future, I think."

"That sounds good to me," I replied. "But maybe you need more balance in your life. Do you ever unplug? Take a break?"

He gave me a guilty look. "Yes, I know. I should."

"If you have all this money, you should invest some of it. And I don't mean in the quote/unquote financial sector. Buy a nice cottage on a big lake. With a long driveway and no cell phone coverage. And come up north at least once a month."

He stopped in his tracks and looked out over Lake Ontario. "Zora? You're right. I'll do it. Will you come and visit me?"

Are you kidding? Visit a tall, distinguished-looking, fascinating man in his lakeside getaway? "As long as I can bring the dog," I replied.

We didn't start out making a pact of secrecy or anything. We just didn't tell anyone. And then it became sort of fun. Had Darius escaped the city unnoticed? Had Rocco and I turned a weekend errand into dinner at the lake without drawing attention?

Unfortunately, this particular weekend was not going to work out. Darius said, "I can't make it. I'm in San Francisco, and it will be a few more days until I fly home."

I decided to keep the conversation short and save all my news until I could see him in person. "Enjoy California," I said, "Take care."

I carried on with my household chores, taking a heaping laundry basket down to the main floor and filling up the washer. My machine had a mind of its own and always seemed to take about an hour to finish a cycle, so I had more than enough time to walk Rocco around the block and warm up some spicy Indian food left over from a couple of nights ago.

I let the dog out into the small backyard while I hung out the laundry. As soon as I'd bought the building, I'd fixed up the rear access to the place. There had been three small gravel and weed-choked parking spots. I'd left one, and hired a guy to build a solid eight-foot privacy fence around the remaining two spots, turning them into a pretty lawn with a few loads of topsoil and some grass seed. I'd also added a two-story deck. The staff could use the lower one at lunchtime, and upstairs I could easily get outside to barbecue or lounge around.

The finishing touch had been a nice long clothesline. I loved drying things outside and tonight I'd hung up a set of sheets, a towel, and several pairs of multi-colored tights and mix-and-match tunics. Some lingerie and a small dog blanket finished the job.

Laundry finished and squirrels evicted from the yard, we were enjoying a peaceful Friday night at home. I sipped on a glass of iced tea and patted the dog on my lap as I sat in my favorite armchair and watched the sun set over Main Street. It was so relaxing, and before long the apartment was pitch dark except for the gentle glow of the streetlights.

Suddenly Rocco sat up, at the alert. He began with a low growl but, as usual, this escalated into a fit of barking that was deafening. To my surprise, he headed for the patio door that led out onto the back deck, not to the front door which Marley and others used. I wasn't too worried at first. I took a quick look, squinting into the darkness, and didn't see anything in my little yard. Once in a blue moon, bears came into town. Deer as well. Roc would certainly let me know if he caught the scent of any of those types of visitors hanging around.

I said, "There's nothing! Be quiet! No barking!"

But as I leaned over to give him a comforting scratch behind the ears, I caught a glimpse of light. It looked like The Prince was right after all. Someone was out there. But why would anyone need a flashlight in town? The streetlamps were perfectly adequate for an evening stroll.

Then I screamed, "No!"

I ran out on the deck, forcing Rocco to stay indoors where I could still hear him guarding his brains out. But I was making more noise than him by then.

Someone on foot had tossed not one but two lit Molotov cocktails over the fence and into my yard. It took me a second to see how poor their aim was, and that they hadn't come close to hitting the office window. But it was still bad news. The building was safe, for the moment. But the second bomb had got tangled in my laundry and the better part of my current wardrobe was on fire. My collection of tights! My tunics, from animal prints to inspirational slogans, to flowing colorful fabrics! All ablaze.

As everything hit the ground in a tangle of sheets, polyester, lycra, and leaping flames, I knew I had to do something quickly or things would get much worse.

I ran inside to get my phone and called 911, yelling, "There's a huge fire behind the newspaper office. Hurry, please hurry!"

I grabbed the small fire extinguisher from the hallway outside the kitchen and sprinted downstairs. Who cared if I was wearing my striped pajama pants and a fake fur wrap over a skimpy camisole? I headed outside in flip-flops and sprayed the edge of the fire as it crawled along the grass towards the deck. I was relieved to hear sirens already, and wasn't even remotely sorry to see the firefighters take an ax to the back gate a minute later.

I know it sounds cold-blooded, but I did have the presence of mind to take the phone out of my robe pocket and get a few pictures before the firebombs burned themselves out. But hey, I had a business to run.

It didn't take the crew long to get the blaze under control, and I shivered as I stood on the deck watching the action. My heroes. It could have been a terrible night if the fire department hadn't arrived so quickly. If the flames had spread to my building and then to my neighbors'. I shook my head to banish the thought. What a nightmare!

I tried to ignore the fact that mosquitoes were swarming me, attacking my face and neck, and biting through my clothing. I guess it was marginally cooler in the shade of the deck, where I was standing to watch the firefighters at work. I stayed put because I was pretty sure that Arni Korhonen would stop by and I wanted to speak to him.

By now I was more angry than scared. I wanted this mayor-killing arsonist found. I also decided to talk to the reporters in the morning, even though it was now the weekend. We needed a longer list of suspects, that's for sure.

8

I woke up at the usual time despite the excitement and trauma of the night before. The sun was up, and the air was cool. Although everything smelled like an old campfire. Why was that scent so entrancing when you were camping, and sort of nauseating indoors? It was made worse by the smoke lingering in my long hair. Maybe it was time for a change. Maybe a short haircut would make a statement. Something bristly and no-nonsense.

I made a quick cup of coffee and stepped out onto the deck, gazing down sadly at the scene of the fire. The skeleton of a lawn chair was guarding the lumpy corpse of my former clothing. I made a mental list of the places in town that sold underwear. It was short. The price you pay for small-town living. Friendly, scenic, fun, but difficult to find underwear. Tights and shirts would be easier.

I wondered what the response would be if I just kept washing and wearing my remaining outfits in sequence? Would anyone even care? Something to think about.

Fortunately, the sporty clothing I wore for my walks was still around. I got dressed, put Roc on his leash, and headed out the front door. Setting a quick pace, I let my mind wander. I got many brainwaves on the streets of Williamsport, almost as many as in the shower, the true source of all genius. I hoped a few insights would wash over me today.

I decided it was useless to fret over the fire. Surely the same person was behind that disaster and the mayor's killing. I just needed to focus on a single train of thought and also be open to any possibilities. Clearly, it wasn't straightforward or Arni would have made an arrest already. I figured I could make a positive contribution to the investigation, regardless of what he might think. And if anything useful came to mind, I would tell him.

I headed further along the main street, thinking I would go as far as Highway 60 and then turn around. It was fresh and quiet in the rosy morning sunlight. The streetscape stretched in front of me, looking like a postcard. Or should I say an Instagram post?

Beautiful hanging baskets and sidewalk planters were blooming in bright shades of pink, mauve, and white. The buildings looked quaint and tidy, with awnings over the windows, top floor as well as street level. Wherever there was a large enough expanse of brick between the second-story window openings, there was spectacular Group of Seven street art. They may have been replicas, but they were larger than life and added a unique artistic touch to the street.

I was setting a good pace and had motored through a few blocks. But my heart sank as I saw a tourist coming out of a motel walking a cute little shih tzu. They headed towards us and I sighed.

Rocco presented such a lovely picture. Bright eyes, short curly hair. I continued to keep him clipped in a puppy cut with no poodle flourishes. There was no way I was going to be combing out fluffy ears or tying bows in a topknot. It was embarrassing enough putting a coat on him so he wouldn't freeze in the winter. But that dog was oh, so deceptive.

Here we go, I thought.

The other dog-walker was a plump, middle-aged blond woman wearing flowered capris and a pink fleece sweater. She smiled and said, "What a cute dog!"

I immediately told her, "He doesn't get along well with other dogs."

Right on cue, she replied, "Oh, mine loves all kinds of dogs. I'm sure it will be fine."

Before I could respond, she'd let her small puffy pet come too close. Couldn't she see the 'war tail'? For several years, I had been mystified as to why Rocco looked playful and friendly, and other dogs immediately attacked him. Then careful observation had revealed the war tail.

It was a classic bait and switch. Rocco displayed himself as the picture of innocence to humans. But to dogs, the war tail, arced over his back and vibrating slightly, said "Bring it." The reality, his true personality, was exposed to them.

Sure enough, the shih tzu exploded in a frenzy of snarls and yaps, going for Rocco's throat. Following the usual script, its owner was horrified, exclaiming, "Oh my gosh, I'm so sorry. She's never done that before! Misty! No! Stop that! Bad dog!"

Same old, same old. I'd lost track of how many times I had seen the identical canine battle scene unfold. I always felt sorry for the other dog, getting a good scolding when it was all Rocco's fault.

I smiled, and said, "No problem, have a nice day," and dragged The Prince further north down the sidewalk.

Once I had reached the highway and turned around to head home for breakfast, I decided to text the reporters. We had a system where one of us covered all weekend events on a rotating basis. If it was your turn, you went out to festivals, fairs, and special events all over our coverage area, taking snaps and getting information for stories. Otherwise, you were free. I rarely contacted my staff on their days off. This weekend Brady was up. I knew it was pretty quiet, and that he only had an artists' studio tour to cover.

I phrased the message carefully, telling them, "I know it's the weekend. Ignore this if you want. I have photos of the fire at my place. Want to talk about our list. Lattes on my tab at 10. Optional."

As I finished up my walk, I had one word on my mind. Boyfriend.

In fact, I could think of two boyfriends who I wanted to know more about. I couldn't remember who Olivia had been socializing with in the last year or two. Could one of those young men have been carrying a torch? Had he found out her secret and decided to clear the path for himself to have a more serious romance with her?

As well, I wanted to know more about the doctor's son. Was Jordan Phipps really seeing Tyler Aston? Was he really in law school as Marley had said?

I was pretty sure the reporters would have some insight into all this. They didn't seem to miss much in this town.

I got home, had some more coffee and a yogurt with cereal. Then, I dragged everything out of my closet and the middle drawer of my chest of drawers and threw it on the bed.

Except for dresses. I had to draw the line somewhere, and that line was weddings and funerals. I would not be wearing dresses on any other days.

I used to be thin. Even willowy. I could eat anything and still stayed in top form. I'm not taking credit for that. It was genetic, and the same ancestors who gave my face a bit of the hawk gave me long limbs and a fast metabolism. Now, however, that had changed. Partly it was a few extra pounds, partly force of gravity.

First of all, I had curves where I never had any before, and no sooner had I got used to that then they all started to sag. I still considered myself fit, due to my explorations around the town at all hours with The Prince. But it didn't seem to help the general shape of things. I knew I could still rock a tight pair of jeans and a low-cut t-shirt but usually I couldn't be bothered.

The boots that I favored helped to showcase my legs. So far, they hadn't let me down, as my legs were long and a decent shape. My other vanity was my blue eyes. They were more on the narrow and icy side than round and friendly, and I'd splurged on laser surgery a few years ago. No glasses required. The procedure also let me continue to indulge a sunglasses habit. Which was cheaper than the boot habit.

Looking at the pile of clothing on my bed was sort of depressing. I needed to package up some things for the charity shop and drop them off on my walk tomorrow morning. But the question was, did I have enough stuff to wear, and could I postpone a shopping excursion?

In the 'keep' pile, I laid out two pairs of black tights, one capri-length and one full-length. So far so good. I had enough underwear for three days, plus an extra sports bra. Also good.

I untangled three more pairs of tights. One set looked like camo. What had ever possessed me to buy those? Straight to the donation bin. Of the other two, one was lined with a layer of fuzzy material and would be no use until the fall. I stuck them back in the drawer. The final candidate passed my selection criteria. A floral pattern with fuchsia and turquoise colors.

The tops were a nightmare. I found three t-shirts that brought back memories of trips out west and to the States. Memphis, Banff, and Fernie would be going to new homes. Also, I didn't think I needed five different-colored Williamsport Fun Run event t-shirts. I kept a purple and a red, and set aside the others.

I grabbed a couple of nice blouses and a plaid shirt and hung them back up, in case I ever broke down and wore jeans again. I discarded two longer shirts. They would work with tights and were made of nice material, but one made me look like a blimp and in the other I resembled a stuffed bratwurst. I picked up a third. It had a peplum that made my behind look enormous, so it could go as well.

In the 'keep' pile I was left with one flowing dressy top, silvery, with a cowl neck and split sleeves. Plus, two longer tunics. One was white, with a loose empire waist, a shirt collar, and navy-blue buttons down the front. The other was a neutral ecru, in a loose-knit, basic caftan shape.

This would be fine. No shopping needed at the moment. Maybe I'd treat myself when I'd accomplished my goal. And the person who had ended the life of Mayor Phipps was behind bars.

9

"Thank you both so much. I know it's the weekend," I said. "I'll try not to make a habit of it."

They both nodded seriously, even though I'd meant it as a joke. Oh well. Everyone knew that millennials liked to have a decent work-life balance. I'd read an article about hiring and keeping millennials happy on the job. It had become my HR manual, as I certainly didn't want to lose either of these two.

The term millennials referred to people born towards the end of the last century. Fulfilling another of their traits, the tech-savvy Brady asked me to airdrop my fire photos to his laptop and he went ahead and updated the website then and there.

I asked him to make sure to credit the members of the fire department for their swift response and to point out how dangerous the situation had been. And begged him to not make any references to my presence at the death of Mayor Phipps. Any connection between Fred's death and the arson was a theory that I didn't want to gain traction in the public eye. Even though it had given me a good scare.

Olivia asked for the photos as well, and said she'd post something on Instagram later. I said, "You can make it humorous if you want. Most of my clothes went up in flames."

"But you and Rocco are OK?" she asked.

"Thank you. We are."

They looked at me expectantly. I had already written our list from yesterday on the whiteboard: Councilor Leona Riggs and her offspring, Sonny. Ollie Hanson. The building-permit people.

"Any other candidates for our list? I can add a couple," I began. "But first. Well, I'll just spit it out. Olivia, do you think that there is any chance a former boyfriend of yours might have gone after Fred?"

Their jaws dropped. I guessed millennials shocked easily. I thought it was a perfectly logical question.

Olivia sounded huffy as she replied, "No. I don't think I would have been going out with a murderer, for one thing. Secondly, no one knew."

"But Brady kicked you and suggested you confide in me. That means he knew. Maybe someone else did as well?"

She looked embarrassed. "That was just a total coincidence. Brady was down in Toronto to see a Jays game and saw us in Fred's car, stopped at a streetlight. I told him the truth and trusted him not to tell a soul."

We both looked over at Brady, who raised his hands and said, "Whoa. Don't look at me like that. I never said a thing. To anybody."

Olivia looked over at me and said, "I believe him. He never even said anything to me afterward, no teasing or joking around or anything."

"OK, but are they still around? Guys you might have gone out with, even briefly?"

"Nope. I only went out for any length of time with one person, and he's visiting his sister in Australia. For a year. In case you haven't noticed, the selection is pretty slim around here."

"You'll get no argument from me," I said, shaking my head. The pair of them looked at me as if I were an alien. They'd probably faint if I ever told them about Darius.

"OK, on the same subject, should we add Tyler Aston to the list?"

"Jordan's boyfriend?" asked Brady. "Sure. I've only met him once and didn't get any bad vibes off him. He seemed sort of boring to me. But who knows?"

Olivia sniffed, "Well, I find it quite funny that he's taking a law degree. He had quite the side hustle in high school. Even though it's legal now, it wasn't then."

"Very interesting," I replied. "I'll add him. If he's moved on from weed to other products, he might have a motive. Say Fred found out and threatened him. He'd lose everything, it wouldn't be just about Jordan."

Olivia said, "Well, as much as I don't like him, I don't think he's selling anything anymore. Not around here at least."

I added Tyler Aston anyway.

I said, "The next idea I want to run by you is concerning Councilor Rigg. I heard a few months ago that her kid, the drunk driver, had a bush party while the councilor was out of town. It got out of hand, and someone driving by called both the police and fire department. But, surprisingly, no charges were laid. They had no permit for the fire, there was supposedly underage drinking, and the music could be heard for miles. People also said the kids were firing off guns."

Brady observed, "This is reminding me of what we said yesterday about bylaw enforcement. If she isn't the killer, we should definitely look into a story on why this lady and her family seem to be coated with Teflon."

Olivia said, "Sure. Keep them both. The mother and son."

She continued, "I have two to add. One is silly and likely not worth following up. But I managed to get my parents talking yesterday at dinner and they came up with a good suggestion."

"Great," I said. "Let's have it."

"Well, I hate to say the word 'bylaw' again, but you know how we have a regulation about skateboarding on the sidewalk and in the small parks downtown? Well, I heard that all of a sudden the bylaw is being enforced and there are a few hot-heads at the high school who were making threats on social media."

I added 'angry skateboarders' to the list.

"By the way," I noted. "These crime-solving sessions are proving quite useful for story ideas. Maybe we should have a monthly meeting where we just exchange rumors about our fellow citizens." I was only half-joking and I think they knew it.

Olivia spoke up again, "The last idea I have comes from my dad. You know The Penalty Box? The bar out by the highway? He said he heard that they've been serving after hours and the mayor already went out there and tried to talk to the owner. The guy went off on Fred, banged things around and accused Fred of acting like a fascist. That sort of thing."

I could well believe this had occurred. The owner of The Penalty Box was Moose Logan. But he did not have the temperament of his namesake. He should have been called Honey Badger Logan, or maybe Wild Boar Logan. He had a terrible temper, the opposite of the jovial bartender cliché. Nevertheless, people said he was extremely funny and generous to a fault. I guess that's why he had stayed in business for so long.

Brady said, "I like that rumor. A lot. It's an actual conflict between a person and the mayor, not a secondary connection like most of the others."

I parked the marker and sat down. "Thank you both so much. I appreciate your time today and I think this gives us a bit to go on. We'll talk further on Monday about whether we want to follow up with any of these ideas. Also, the website and social media work are much appreciated."

They stood up. Brady stretched and Olivia reached down for her large bag and slung it over her shoulder. "Have a good weekend, Zora," she said.

"You too. And safe travels, Brady."

I gazed back up at the whiteboard and took a hard look at the name Ollie Hanson. I thought a little drive in the country was in store for me today.

Everyone knew that the Phipps residence was located down a network of backroads that led off Ravenscliffe Road. Hopefully, Hanson, the angry neighbor, would have his name on his mailbox so I could see whether he lived on the left or the right side of the late mayor. And his dog Harper.

I went upstairs, checked for any NSP action from the Nasty Small Poodle I shared my home with, and made a peanut butter sandwich to take in the car. I filled up my water bottle and said, "Let's go, Rocco. Where's the car?"

He leaped up and did his three-legged run down the stairs, barking and whining until I caught up with him. I went to the back door of the office and picked Roc up to carry him out to the car. The yard was such a mess. If it was quiet on Monday, I'd get Barbara to make some calls for me. I badly needed a property cleanup and a new gate.

I was extremely relieved that the fire had not reached my vehicle. I'd had various cars over the years but was settled in for the long term with a black RAV4. Totally dependable. For longer trips, Rocco always traveled in his crate, but for little jaunts around town, I often let him ride shotgun. Although given where we were going, I probably shouldn't even use that term.

10

I had the windows down a bit, and that enticed the dog to stay put in the passenger seat with his nose in the breeze, instead of slinking over to sit on my lap. It was such a beautiful day.

I drove slowly through Williamsport, across the Highway II overpass to Ravenscliffe Road, and headed out of town. Numerous gravel roads led off in either direction and I kept going for a little while. The maple leaves were almost fluorescent green, tamaracks had pale green lace fronds once again, and the woods were filled with new ferns and trilliums.

Eventually, I turned off onto the road where Mayor Phipps had lived. The back roads outside Williamsport were a varied mix of dwellings, from large timber frame showplaces to hunting camps from an earlier era. I slowed as I approached the Phipps residence. It was a suburban-style raised bungalow that had been updated with stonework and charcoal colored siding. I took a good look at the mailboxes and sure enough, next door there was one marked Hanson.

Ollie Hanson's driveway was pretty full with a variety of vehicles. It was impossible to tell if any of them ran. In fact, it was hard to say what color they might have been, under the rust. And it would take a careful inspection to determine if each truck or car had four tires. I counted two pickups, a tractor with the snowblower still on, and what looked like the relic of a Hyundai Pony.

Anyway, I decided it would be safer and more courteous to park at the side of the road and pulled over onto the shoulder. I figured Mr. Hanson probably didn't own a dog as no pets had featured in the anecdote Brady had shared at our meeting.

I left Rocco perched on the console between the two front seats. He was on the alert, his black nose avidly sniffing the air. The windows were open enough to give him some cool airflow but, hopefully, closed enough to prevent an escape. I somehow didn't think that Ollie Hanson would have any appreciation for a nasty, small poodle. On the other hand, as long as Rocco didn't do his business on Ollie's lawn, maybe things would be fine.

I closed the door and headed across the road and up the driveway. I called out, "Mr. Hanson?" If he was in his yard on this gorgeous spring day, I could just chat outside with him here.

Ollie Hanson had an older house, almost a cabin in size. It was covered in weathered board-and-batten siding and had a small screened porch. An old outhouse was perched at the bush line. The main house was situated in the center of a small shady clearing. A bit of sun filtered through the branches of the hardwoods and spruce that surrounded it.

Sure enough, other than the boneyard of vehicles, the whole property was neat as a pin. The homes in this area looked like they were on five-acre lots, so Mayor Phipps really had let his dog roam. I was starting to side with Ollie Hanson before I had even met him. Mind you, I don't think I would necessarily have turned to a gun to solve the problem.

I was slowly strolling up the driveway when all of a sudden there was a huge commotion in the woods to my right. Loud yelling broke the silence of the countryside. I could hear something crashing through the bush, birds shrieked, and a couple of squirrels darted across the lawn to the far side, ran up an old poplar, and added their chattering voices.

I stopped in my tracks and looked across the small yard.

Suddenly, a short scrawny man with thinning gray hair burst out of the forest. He took a panicked look around and sprinted right past me. As he went by, I could see that he was wearing a baggy, filthy, formerly-white tank top that did nothing to cover the hundreds of blackfly bites on his torso. He also had on scanty denim cutoffs, heavy wool socks, and steel-toed work boots.

Before I could properly process this, two things happened. Looking to my right, at the man I assumed to be Ollie Hanson, I was astounded to see him open the back door of the RAV, leap into the back seat, slam the door and crouch down on the floor.

I whipped my head around to my left in time to see a large black bear, followed by a cub not much bigger than Rocco, making a beeline right for me. I also heard Ollie click the locks on my RAV doors. Before I could catch my breath, I heard Roc in full voice and realized he was standing at my feet screaming at the bear. I thought he was wasting his time with the war tail.

I came to my senses, picked him up, ran back to the RAV, and popped the dog up onto the roof. I darted around to the passenger side, putting the vehicle between me and Mama Bear. I got one foot on top of the front tire and hoisted myself up onto the hood of the car. I began waving my arms and making some noise of my own. I didn't know who to holler at first, Ollie Hanson, or the bear. It probably didn't make any difference.

The bear seemed to be re-thinking her strategy. She stopped short of the SUV, thank goodness, as I'm pretty sure she could have polished off both Rocco and me in short order. She reared up on her hind legs and huffed and snorted. This was still not good, but better than a full-on assault.

Then the worst possible thing happened. Rocco slalomed down the windshield and across the hood and flew down to the ground.

Gaining traction on the gravel, he took off towards the bear, arpeggios of sharp barks piercing the air. "No! Roc, come! Come here," I yelled.

Both bears headed for the woods with Rocco snapping at their heels. I was pretty sure that wouldn't have concerned them, but I could well believe that they might have wanted to get away from the barking. Regardless, my precious Prince Rocco was long gone. All I could imagine was the bear finally reaching her limit, turning around and giving him a mighty swat. Right before feeding him to her cub for an afternoon snack. He thought he was so fast on his dainty little feet, but he'd be no match for an angry bear.

I turned on Ollie in fury. "Open this door right now," I screamed. "Get out, get out!"

He emerged sheepishly, saying, "I'm so very sorry. I was out picking wild leeks and, all of a sudden, the bear was right beside me. I ran."

"No kidding," I replied, eyeing him up and down.

He got a bit defensive, and said, "Well, I wasn't exactly expecting company. Excuse me. I will go and get changed." He had a slight Scandinavian lilt to his speech that I might have found charming under other circumstances.

"No, you will not. When you opened my car, you let my little dog out. Now he's lost in the woods likely being eaten by the bear that you brought over here."

"I didn't bring it! I was trying to get away from it! I've always been afraid of them. There it was, as close to me as you are."

I backed up and said, "Tough. You can just go and get your

gun and help me find my dog. Dead or alive," I added with a catch in my voice.

He looked horrified, "Gun! I would never own a gun. I guess I can get my ski poles. But I'm not sure that would do much good."

I thought he was probably right, but I just ignored him and headed into the bush.

So much for rumors. If Ollie wouldn't pick up a shotgun to defend himself against a bear that he was deathly afraid of, I doubted that he was the sort of person to shoot Fred Phipps. Dog or no dog. Although I thought I could hear the goose honking in the backyard.

I walked back and forth in the woods for at least an hour, calling Rocco's name and hoping I would see his small furry face around every bend. I could hear Ollie calling for him too, out behind the cabin. The longer I searched, the more upset I became. Soon I was sobbing and, by the time I gave up, I figured I probably didn't look much better than Ollie. I was heartbroken at the thought of losing my little wooly Prince.

As I approached the car, I pulled out a tissue and wiped my eyes. In all the excitement, the back door of the RAV had been left open. I hoped it had some kind of high-tech gadget that had prevented the battery from running down.

Suddenly I had to laugh through my tears. I shook my head in disbelief. As I approached the RAV, a small beige figure with a long pointy muzzle and large black eyes popped up. He shook his head, flapped his ears, and stretched. While I had been desperately searching the woods, feeding a wide variety of insects, and crying inconsolably, Rocco had apparently been having a nap.

I dashed over, closed the back door, and got into the driver's seat. Rocco jumped up on my lap and licked my face. I didn't even make him stop, just hugged him. Once I calmed down, I could see the evidence of his bear hunt. His fur, which was about an inch long, was completely tangled with brambles, dead leaves, and old twigs. I didn't care. I would be perfectly happy to sit on the sofa all night and brush him.

I tooted the horn a couple of times, turned around in Ollie's driveway, and headed back to civilization.

11

S unday passed without incident. Although I did sneak downstairs to look at the whiteboard and its list of possible suspects.

So far, we had six.

Councilor Leona Rigg.

Her son, aptly named Sonny Rigg.

Jordan Phipps.

Her boyfriend, Tyler Aston.

The bylaw officer, whose name I couldn't recall for the life of me.

Moose Logan, The Penalty Box bar owner.

I left off Richard Park and, reluctantly, erased the entry for Ollie Hanson.

Although Mr. Hanson was working his way off the suspect list and into my good books. While I was in the meeting room, I'd heard tapping on the front door. When I went out to see who was there, I saw that it was Ollie. Fully-clothed and bearing a bouquet of grocery store carnations. I admit I wasn't too friendly, but he apologized for his behavior the day before and handed me the flowers. And a Ziplock bag full of wild leeks.

As he turned to go, he stopped and said, "I never asked you why you were at my house in the first place."

I sighed. "You might as well come in."

Our office floor plan was pretty basic. At the front was a large bright room where Barbara Stevens held court. It had a little reception seating area with a couch and two armchairs set up around a coffee table. Then, a long hallway led past the doorways of three dark cave-like rooms that provided office space for me and the reporters, and a staff washroom. Finally, at the rear of the building, there was another spacious sunny room that we used for editorial meetings and more private visits.

I led Ollie into the meeting room and waved at the whiteboard. "I wanted to meet you. We heard that you were angry at Fred Phipps about his dog. I was going to see if I could find out whether you killed him."

He actually laughed. "No, Ms. Flynn. I did not kill the mayor."

"Please. Call me Zora," I said automatically. I hated being called Ms. Flynn, or especially Mrs. Flynn.

"Very well. Zora. I guess you deduced that since I wouldn't shoot the bear, I would not be likely to kill either Fred or his dog."

"Pretty much," I acknowledged. "You can see the gap on the board where I erased your name."

He nodded. "That's a pretty good list. I don't know any of them personally. But you are missing a bunch of people."

"What?" I was surprised. "Really?"

A smile widened across his wrinkled face, crinkling his light blue eyes. "Politicians. Fred and I got along quite well, as neighbors. Other than for the dog business." He chuckled at his play on words and then continued. "But we didn't have enough in common to become real friends. We had really different ideas when it comes to politics."

"In what way?"

"I believe that many politicians are self-centered, egotistical people looking for power or money. Very cynical, I know."

I couldn't really argue with the man. I thought he was realistic, rather than cynical.

He carried on, "But Fred was very committed. He truly felt as though being a politician was the highest form of public service. Not a greedy or dishonest bone in his body."

Well, that matched everything I had ever heard about the man. For the first time in all the drama and chaos that had accompanied Fred's death, I felt a pang of sadness. His loss was a real blow to the community.

Meanwhile, Ollie had one other comment of interest, "But I cannot say the same thing about most of his visitors."

"Visitors?"

"There were always people coming and going from his place. Politicians, most of them."

"Like who?"

Unfortunately, the names that Ollie rhymed off formed a fairly complete catalog of our local politicians. Fred had obviously been open-minded in his friendships. All parties and all levels of government were represented. There was no way I could add all of those people to our list.

But I was also convinced that Ollie had given us a good tip. The reporters and I had left a big gap in our list. We'd omitted the very individuals that Fred spent the most time with.

I had one other question. "I also heard you were annoyed that the bylaw officer wouldn't respond."

"True enough," said my visitor. "I thought I should be able to call and complain, and that the mayor would be treated like any other citizen. I guess I was wrong."

I stood up. "Thanks for stopping by, Ollie. And for the flowers. They'll brighten the place up."

He replied, "Sorry we got off on the wrong foot, and I'm glad you got your pup back."

He walked back out the door and I locked up after him. Then I put the flowers in a vase on Barbara's desk and went back to my office to continue sleuthing.

I looked at my desk and shook my head. What a mess. I started to idly make stacks of paper that I could go through in more detail later. Sadly, I knew my email inbox was in the same state. Electronic communication hadn't really lived up to its promise to reduce my workload.

Tomorrow was Monday. A big day in the weekly newspaper world. Story topics would be finalized and written, pictures selected, and content would flow to Barbara for page layout. Ideally, we'd have something to add to the online material we'd already published about Mayor Phipps.

Not to mention, the Mayor's funeral would be tomorrow.

I had a full week of publisher duties ahead, with our summer supplement just about ready for printing. As well, we were co-sponsoring a fundraiser for the hospital foundation and that was approaching fast.

But somehow, I would have to find the time to carry on with our investigation. I felt that a cloud would be over me, dogging my footsteps and darkening my thoughts, until the person who killed Fred, and thought I knew their name, was in custody.

I could think of one logical step to take. It sure would be helpful to know how many of our suspects were at the Legion at the time of the murder. I needed to think of someone who I could sit down with for a quiet chat. Someone I could trust not to spread the word that the Williamsport Whistle staff was investigating crime on the side.

I leaned back in my chair and tried to recall the crowd of women who had been in the ladies' room at the Legion when I'd retreated there to rinse out the sleeve of my shirt and collect my thoughts. A smile spread across my face. Tamara Pellegrino.

Tamara was a cute dumpling of a woman who often joined Marley and me after work for coffee or a drink. She had curly, short blond hair and wide green eyes and told hilarious stories about her four young children. And although we would never tell him, she often had a few anecdotes about her long-suffering husband as well. As a bonus, Tamara was the civilian receptionist at the police station and knew how to be discreet.

I picked up my phone, tapped her number, and left a text message. I knew Sundays were really hectic for Tamara, but maybe she'd find a minute to ring me back. In the meantime, I went online and created a complete list of every politician who served our area. And their employees.

The more I thought about Ollie's point, the more complex the scenario got. Let's say there was a slim chance that Fred, despite his reputation, had angered another political figure. That meant there was an equal chance that he had somehow enraged a Town Hall staffer, or someone who worked for either of our provincial or federal reps. I went ahead and added anyone I could think of, or who I could find a reference to online.

At the same time, I looked up the name of the bylaw officer. Finally, I could add it to the list. Carlton Miner.

If I was going to get a few minutes of Tamara's time, I wanted to make the most of it.

12
_____

I was in luck. Just a few minutes later, Tamara wrote back that she was out on her own picking up a few things at the grocery store. I asked her if she could meet me at The Penalty Box. The text that I got back contained a few question marks and a beer stein emoji, but it seemed like she was up for it.

I gave Rocco a biscuit, told him to guard, and headed over to the west side of town where the bar was. Although, like most of the local hospitality spots, The Penalty Box was just as much a family restaurant as a sports bar. While they did have lots of big TVs, a good selection of beers, and Happy Hour specials, they also did kids' pizza parties and minor hockey banquets.

When I walked in out of the bright sun, I had to blink a couple of times to let my eyes adjust. The Penalty Box had a nice mix of booths, smaller tables, and dining tables. And not a bad seat in the house when it came to watching sports on TV. There was a long bar down the left side that provided lots more seating, and then several open areas divided by half walls throughout the large space.

Plus, lots and lots of hockey memorabilia. Equipment from

various eras was festooned from the walls and ceilings, interspersed with signed photos of the greats, local and national.

Tamara was already waiting for me in a wooden booth with cushiony bright red vinyl seats, a frosty Coke in front of her. She was wearing a Blue Jays t-shirt, jeans, and a denim vest. She had tried to tuck her blonde curls into a hairband, but some of the tendrils had escaped. I smiled and sat down opposite her. "Thanks so much for meeting me," I said. "It's great to see you."

"Well, yeah. We didn't really get a chance to visit at the Legion the other night. But why here?"

"I'll tell you in a second. Just let me order something. If I get the nachos, will you eat some?"

"There's a slight chance I can help you out with them."

I also ordered a light beer and vowed to only consume half of it.

"I guess both of us have been busy in the last few days," she commented.

"You can say that again. First the mayor, then the fire. Then the bear."

"Bear? What bear?"

I regaled her with my Ollie Hanson story which had us both laughing like crazy until my beer and nachos arrived. Tamara was well-acquainted with Rocco, and she said, "I can just see him curling up in the sun for a siesta while you're out searching for him."

"That's The Prince for you," I agreed.

I picked up a crispy hot nacho chip loaded with cheese, onions, and peppers, and demolished it in a couple of bites. The beer hit the spot, too. But I felt I should get to the point. In a sneaky roundabout way.

"So, I haven't talked to Arni in a couple of days. Do you know if they've made any progress?"

"Well, I probably shouldn't say."

I let that hang there for a minute, and then Tamara continued anyway. "But I'm guessing that it's a 'no'. It took them all of Friday to get statements from everyone who was at the Legion. And I don't think anything has happened since. I mean they all have assignments, and they're working, I just don't think they have anyone."

I nodded, ate some more food, and pushed the plate across the table towards her. "I wanted to know if I can pick your brain."

She stopped with a nacho halfway to her mouth. "Zora. You know I can't say anything!"

"No, it's not that. I understand. But Brady, Olivia, and I have been making lists of story ideas, things we can maybe pursue in the next week or so. Now, I'm not asking you what the officers have said. I just want to know your own personal recollections of Thursday night."

"Hmm. I don't see anything wrong with that. I already told Arni everything I can remember."

I slid a printout of my big list over to her and said, "I have only one question. Of those people, how many did you see at the Legion that night? Or maybe you can just cross off anyone who wasn't there."

"OK, I can do that." She fished around in her enormous purse and pulled out a pen. She sat for a few minutes, studying the list of names: politicians, staffers, our whiteboard suspects. Then she set down her pen.

"What?" I asked. "Is there a problem?"

"No, not at all."

"But you didn't cross... Oh." The lightbulb had gone off. I took a long drink of light beer.

"Correct," she said. "All of these people were in the room at one time or another."

"Moose?" I asked in an undertone.

She nodded, "Yes. He was dropping off his girlfriend. She's a card-carrying Tory. He had a drink at the bar and chatted with some people."

"Sonny Rigg?" I asked in disbelief.

"Yup. His mother, the councilor, was helping to organize the meeting. She was carrying in boxes at the start of the event. He helped her, then they asked him to stay and run the sound system."

I was feeling sort of incompetent. I mean I had been in the same room for a lot of the evening, and I hadn't noticed half of the people on the list. Mind you, I didn't know them all. "Tamara, do you actually know all these people?"

She laughed, "Yes, I really do. Part of it comes from growing up here. Some of it's from the job."

"Wow."

"And Zora? This is not a list of people to contact for a news story, correct?"

"Well, I hope we'll be writing about one of them someday soon," I replied. At this, we both had to laugh.

"But no," I admitted. "I'm feeling like I need to be pro-active about this situation. We're doing as much as we can to get the word out on the website, and then in this week's paper, that I didn't see or hear anything that could identify the murderer. Because it's true. However, when someone tried to burn my building down, I figured the message hadn't quite gotten through. Until Fred's killer is caught, I'll be looking over my shoulder every waking minute."

I left Tamara to work on the nachos by herself and headed for the restroom. There were quite a few people that I recognized, between my seat and the hallway where the washrooms were located, and they all nodded and smiled at me as I walked by. Funny, I didn't remember this as such a friendly place.

I carried on towards the ladies' room and then I understood.

I could feel a couple of dozen pairs of eyes on me. Taped to the ladies' door was a large piece of paper with a big red 'Z' on it. The men's door was displaying a similar sign, but this one had the capital 'Z' surrounded by a heavy black circle with a stroke through it. Sort of like a No Smoking symbol. Or the Ghostbusters logo.

I laughed out loud and turned back to the bar. I leaned over it and called out to Moose, who was down at the other end, "Thanks so much. Very helpful."

I was glad to have the chance to joke around with the group of drinkers and sports fans who were seated at the bar. One more chance to say I had seen and heard nothing on Thursday night.

Once I was back at my seat, I thanked Tamara for her help, paid the bill, and headed home.

I felt good about our meeting. We weren't any further ahead, but she'd helped me answer my first big question. And it didn't hurt that we could now answer the question as to who had had the 'Opportunity' to kill Mayor Phipps.

Now we could move on to 'Motive' and 'Means.'

And I was extra glad I'd left on a good footing with Moose Logan. Because I certainly planned to be back soon for a little chat.

13

Monday morning marked a big change in the weather as well as the sad occasion of the mayor's funeral. Rain pounded against my windows and blew in sheets down Main Street. I bundled up in my raincoat and flower-patterned rubber boots and called Rocco for his daily walk. He looked up at me from his bed and I caught him muttering, *"You must be joking."*

"Not at all," I said, "Up and at it." He was dragging his feet, but I took him out for a forced march around the block anyway. He had a waterproof coat, but it was really more like a vest. I knew he hated getting rain on his head. But then he was always very fussy about the weather. He only liked bright temperate days and gave me attitude for any walks that might feature rain, sleet, snow, or temperatures that were too cold or too hot. He especially detested slush underfoot. But then, who didn't?

I got him home and dried him with a fluffy royal blue towel while the coffee dripped.

I didn't want to think about the revenge he might take while I was out.

The funeral was set for 9:30, so I stopped in at the office first.

Barbara was there before me. Today she was wearing a cheery red-checked day dress with a white Peter Pan collar, and a fuzzy white cardigan. Somehow, she'd managed to find T-strap white flats. Her thick brunette hair was curling onto her shoulders and was held back on one side with a sparkly barrette. "Hi, Zora," she greeted me. "Miserable weather! I bet Big Rocco hated his walk today."

"Yes. I can imagine two scenarios right now. One. He's lying in his dog bed, curled up, and watching the rain come down. Two. He tore my bed apart and is lying with his damp head right on my pillow."

"Poor little thing," she said. He obviously had her fooled.

"So, Barbara. This morning, before it gets crazy, can you please help me out with the backyard?"

"For sure. I had a quick look. It's a mess, but I don't think it will take too much work to get it fixed up. This rain will actually help. I'll call the guy who built the fence and ask him to repair the gate. If it's OK with you, Jeff and I will do the yard."

Jeff was her boyfriend, and he had a small contracting business.

She continued, "We'll rake it all up, add a few bags of topsoil and some grass seed. It should look normal pretty soon."

"Thanks, that sounds excellent," I said. I could now check one item off my list for today.

"Second thing. Where are we with the Summer Book?" That's what we called the annual free magazine that was distributed in all the local stores and restaurants. It had feature stories on activities and events and, ideally, lots of ads.

"I'm aiming to have it all ready to print by this Friday. I emailed everyone to get the final ads in, and I'll send the proofs out tomorrow. That gives me a couple of days to chase people for approvals. Olivia and Brady have the stories all finished."

"OK, sounds good. Leave the final pages with me over the weekend. We can get it to the printer next Monday."

"Sure. I'll call them this morning and set that up."

I thanked her and headed for the door. I still had the boots on, which were a little lively for a funeral, but I was wearing them anyway. The office was only two blocks from the church, so I planned to walk to the service. Even if I wanted to bother with the car, the chances of getting a parking spot much closer were slim. It made more sense to go on foot.

I zipped up my raincoat, grabbed a big black umbrella from the stand by the door, and set out to pay my respects to Fred Phipps.

I kept my head down as I trudged through the downpour. The streets were lined with cars and it was a steady stream of colorful bobbing umbrellas as I approached the church. Many of the stores I passed had notices taped to their doors, saying that they would be closed this morning due to a funeral.

The church was located at one of the central intersections on Main Street and was a beautiful old red-brick building with a square Norman tower forming the entrance. In the nave, where we would all be seated, there was a beautiful vaulted ceiling lined with dark wood paneling. Stained glass windows were spaced along the walls.

I saw Olivia arrive just ahead of me and, once I was inside, I went and sat with her. I thought it would look better if everyone assumed we were there together from the Williamsport Whistle. She was wearing a selection of black clothes topped by a tiny cardigan with rhinestone buttons and had chosen a black satin hairband. The church was packed, as expected, and latecomers were now standing around at the back and up the side aisles. The crowd had brought the dampness from the rain into the building, but clerestory windows were open to circulate the air.

The proceedings were very moving. Fred Phipps had had a

long life of public service and had also extended personal kindnesses to many. Even though I hadn't been a close friend, it was still a sad occasion. Eulogies were given by a couple of councilors, and the minister read a tribute from Jordan. I felt sorry for her. She was so young to have now lost both parents.

The minister announced that the mayor's ashes would be interred later at a private family gathering and invited us all to join Jordan and her extended family in the church hall for refreshments.

I glanced over at Olivia. She looked pale but had managed to keep her tears at bay. "Do you want to go to the reception?" I asked her quietly.

"Yes, I think so," she replied. We were seated near the back so, eventually, we joined the last of the mourners and proceeded into the spacious hall. It was a bright, pleasant room painted in neutral colors, with oak wainscoting along one wall and a big roll-up window open to the kitchen on another.

Olivia and I stood quietly along one wall and looked around the room. It was packed with people, and I could see many of our suspects. Moose Logan was talking to Marley. Politicians of all stripes seemed to have set aside their differences for the morning and were making small talk with one another.

Arni Korhonen was a vision in his dress uniform, and I spotted a couple of other police officers as well. Their presence was a subtle reminder that Fred had not died a natural death.

It seemed as though being released from the formal confines of the church, and the sadness of the funeral service, had lightened people's spirits. Voices were more boisterous, and I saw a few smiles and laughs around the room as those present allowed themselves to think of something other than their friend's death.

I elbowed Olivia and tilted my head in the direction of the food and drink. Her eyes widened as she saw Tyler Aston discreetly pouring a mickey of vodka into the punch bowl.

"Oh, that's not cool," she whispered. "People won't be expecting it at this hour of the day."

I agreed, and said, "I'm glad we saw him. I would have stuck to coffee anyway, but still. And pastries. I would be happy to eat a few pastries."

We started to walk towards the coffee station but were stopped in our tracks at the sight of Jordan. It seemed as though once the formalities had ended, unlike most people in the room, her mood had darkened. She was crying and looked angry, not sad. In her hand was a glass of punch, and my guess was it wasn't her first drink of the day. Tyler had his arm around her shoulders, but she shrugged it off.

I figured if I could hear her from halfway across the room, everyone else could too. Her voice was raised, and she said, "Just leave me alone."

He said something to her in an undertone, but it had no effect.

"I can say whatever I want. He was my father and he was too young to die. All you cops? I can give you a clue. You should interrogate all the women here. I know he was seeing someone. I bet she lost her mind and shot him."

Olivia looked like she was about to head for the hills, but I murmured, "Don't move. You'll just draw attention to yourself."

We stood stock-still. The room was quiet now, and Jordan glared around the room with her red eyes and tears. I had a moment of panic when she seemed to look right at me. She continued to rant, "I see why you let Zora go. There's no way they were involved. He didn't really like her that much."

I smiled stiffly. It wasn't the time or place to defend myself.

Suddenly she swung around and pointed at Marley, "I bet it was you. He was always talking to you. I saw him go into your office the day before he died."

Someone should tell Jordan that accountants did meet occasionally with their clients. Poor Marley. She looked shocked, and said, "Jordan, no, you're mistaken."

As Jordan leveled a series of colorful allegations at Marley, I turned to Olivia and said, "Now would be a good time. Just walk slowly to the door and don't look back." She did.

Tyler looked like he wanted the floor to open and swallow him, but he managed to get Jordan to walk away and sit on an old Naugahyde couch in one corner. He brought her a coffee and some mini-Danishes, but she glared at him and handed over her punch glass for a refill. He set the stuff down on the end table and did as he was told.

I walked over to the refreshments, got a cup of coffee, and poured a generous serving of punch for Marley. I went over to her and said, "Here. You need this."

She took a sip and gave me a startled look before draining half the glass. "What was that all about! I never!" she exclaimed.

I hid my laugh behind my coffee cup and said, "Oh, don't worry. No one is taking her seriously. But I have a feeling this event is going to become a town legend. Your main problem is going to be your other male clients," I added.

"And why is that?"

"They're going to want the same level of service as Fred.'

I winced as she punched me in the shoulder.

"Holy Toledo," I said, forgetting all about the pain in my bicep. The fireworks weren't over yet.

14

Before it was over, two politicians were bleeding. Carlton Miner, the bylaw officer, had been fired by his boss the fire chief. And Moose Logan had drop-kicked a metal folding chair across the room.

Jordan was passed out on the couch and missed it all.

I couldn't wait to get back to the office. I didn't know what to do first. Write the front-page story for this week's paper or annotate our suspect list.

I had to stop and think about how the uproar had begun. Tyler had got Jordan to keep quiet and sit on the couch, and Olivia had made her escape. Marley was drinking punch, and then...

All hell had broken loose. In the church hall. Whether it was the vodka-laced punch or Jordan's raving, people's tongues were loosened.

A burly man in a brown tweed suit from the 1970s approached Councilor Leona Rigg, shook his finger in her face and shouted, "Without Fred, you people are worthless. Corruption, kickbacks, I don't know what all he was covering up."

Leona Rigg was known as the budget watchdog on council,

and she obviously lived by the same values personally. She was approaching 50 and was as tall as I was, but probably outweighed me by 40 pounds. She still played defense on a women's hockey team, and never held back. She wore a light blue suit from Walmart and dyed her own hair a uniform shade of yellow. I felt she could take the man in the tweed suit, if it came to that.

"Sir, you are out of line, way out of line," she yelled. "Have some respect."

"Respect? Why don't you try to earn some respect?" he returned.

At that, another councilor, Jed McShane, stepped in. I guessed he thought he could act as peacemaker. He tried to grab the man's arm and turn him away from Leona. He turned, all right, and slugged McShane right in the nose. The councilor hit the deck.

Having turned his back on Leona, Mr. Tweed Suit was easy pickings. She hip-checked him and laid him out beside McShane.

Meanwhile, a shoving match had broken out between the Conservative riding association president and the candidates who were still waiting for a re-match. The final vote to determine who would represent the town in the next provincial election had been postponed from last Thursday, and I gathered no new date had yet been set. I could well imagine the frontrunner wanted the soonest time possible. It looked like others disagreed.

The air in the hall was stifling. It was hot and humid, and the crowd was no match for the ventilation system. It made me want to step outside for a few minutes, but there was no way I wanted to miss the dramatics.

The next thing I heard was Leona bellowing, "Sonny!"

I had no idea why that kid wasn't in school, but I thought he was about 16 and had decided to accompany his mother to Fred's funeral. Sonny was easily six feet tall. His hair, unlike that of his mother, was a natural blond, and it hung surfer-style over the collar of his navy blue blazer.

He walked by me and the marijuana fumes almost went to my head. Hot on his tail was Carlton Miner, the bylaw officer.

Carlton was a tall, slim man in late middle age. He had a full head of straight gray hair which he wore in an old-fashioned short cut. It had the appearance and texture of a thatched roof, shorter on the sides and around his ears, and longer on top with a swatch of bangs hanging down over his forehead. He also had a matching thick, bristly mustache that extended out to the edges of his mouth. He was wearing brown slacks and a black sport coat, and had left his fluorescent lime green bylaw officer jacket at home. But he was evidently still on the job.

As Sonny approached his mother, Miner stepped forward. I caught something about, "Smoking on church property," and that was like a match to a fuse.

Suddenly Miner was swarmed by people. The accusations flew.

"Why don't you charge him? Why does he get to run back to Mommy?"

"What about that bush party? That fire was so big it looked like a bomb had gone off. Guns! Drugs! Who knows, probably sex too! They should all have been arrested and thrown in jail."

Leona couldn't get a word in edgewise. I thought she might have a stroke right then and there.

A couple who looked like cottagers in matching Columbia sports shirts and comfort-fit jeans joined the throng. The husband yelled at Miner, "Why did you let our neighbors build that monstrosity of a boathouse? It blocks our view of the sunset. It can't possibly be legal. You were out pestering us every other day when we were building our cottage. But did I ever see you over there? No, I did not!"

Wow. I was going to be able to keep Brady and Olivia busy for a month just based on the comments at this reception. Probably sell a good number of papers, too.

From the latest volley, it sounded like Fred Phipps' dog Harper wasn't the only one getting a free pass. No pun intended. Honestly, why was it so easy to make jokes about dog crap?

Anyway, a group of three women dressed sedately in black dresses and matching pumps pushed their way over to Miner and shouted, "There's two laws for dogs in this town. Councilors and town employees. And the rest of us. I am sick and tired of picking up after Whitmore's dog. He leaves a steaming pile on my front lawn every morning. Every morning!"

Her friend chimed in, "And he comes to my place at dinner time. Really! It's disgusting. We call the town office all the time. And what response do we get? Nothing! Councilor Whitmore does nothing to curb his animal. You do nothing to punish Whitmore."

To my left, a couple of downtown restaurant owners looked like they were getting hot under the collar. They were talking and gesturing wildly. Finally, one turned to Miner and bellowed over the women, "Aren't you supposed to enforce the drinking laws? How come we have to close up on the dot of 2:00 a.m. and The Penalty Box gets to stay open?"

I thought this whole line of talk was very unwise. Sure enough, Moose Logan loomed behind the men. Moose was tall and muscular. He was wearing a gray dress shirt and a formal striped tie under a dressy black vest, with black trousers. He'd put on a few pounds over the years and looked even bigger as a result. His face, darkening in anger, was heavy in the jowls and he had a closely-trimmed black beard and mustache. His hair was buzzed up the sides and gelled in spikes on top. I'm sure he thought it was a mohawk, but his hair was thinning and it looked more like a rooster than anything else.

I heard a scream. Once I looked away from Moose and back to the crowd, I saw that someone had smacked Councilor Whitmore. I figured he'd got too close to someone who had met his dog. Could it really have been those women?

I swiveled my head back to Moose. I finally had the presence of mind to get out my phone and turn the camera on. I even remembered to turn it sideways, so Brady and Olivia wouldn't roll their eyes at my vertical videos. No sooner had I got the camera running when Moose roared, "I obey the law. I always close on time. Who's saying otherwise?" He grabbed a metal folding chair and kicked it, sending it airborne. More screams rang out as people dodged the missile. I turned the video off, smiled in satisfaction, and started walking around taking pictures.

McShane, wild-eyed and disheveled, blood all down the front of his dress shirt.

Leona Rigg yelling at her son. Sonny looking relaxed.

The Conservatives were still at it, and I got a nice group shot. Not one they'd probably want in their brochure.

Arni and the two officers were doing their best to separate the various combatants without actually clearing the room.

Above it all, I heard a whistle. It was Reg Johanson, the fire chief. He raised two fingers to his mouth and let out another shrill tone. The day got even better. It turned out he was also the town's director of protective services, and Carlton Miner's boss.

He said, "I have heard quite enough. This is a scandal. It's disrespectful towards Fred and to the honor of the town. You leave me no choice. Carlton, you're fired!"

The room erupted in cheers.

I was pretty sure that Carlton would be back on the job soon. After all, there were labor laws.

But I was also pretty sure that Carlton had only been doing what he was told. And who might that involve? Was it Fred? And then had someone, either here or absent, taken matters into their own hands? Or had Fred been in the dark? That left several councilors and town staff on the hook. Carlton looked like he was ready to sing.

15

Arni went over to the wall and turned the lights out. Just for a second. People in the room seemed to pause and take a collective breath. He did it a second time and then into the silence he announced, "Thank you. I'm only going to say this once. Everyone will now exit the building. It's a matter of public safety. This is a direct order. Leave the building now."

There was a steel edge to his voice that people didn't often hear, and they gathered up their coats and umbrellas and went out into the rain. I loitered at the back of the crowd finishing my coffee and snagging a couple of the mini-Danishes. But everyone seemed to have returned to normal and they all filed out docilely.

I couldn't wait to get back to the office. The rain was letting up and I didn't even need my umbrella. The bear bells on the front door announced my arrival. Barbara looked up from her computer with a smile, the faint sound of big band music drifting from her speakers. I said, "You may want to join us in the meeting room for a few minutes."

I hung my coat up, put the umbrella in the stand to finish

drying, and exchanged my rubber boots for a pair of Birken-
stocks that I'd left on the boot tray at some point. Well, I have to
admit they were knock-offs. All my serious footwear budget was
allocated to boots.

On my way down the hall, I called out to Brady and Olivia.
As we all made our way into the meeting room, I grabbed a box
of tissues and set it in the middle of the table. "There," I said.
"You'll thank me for that shortly."

Ten minutes later, we were all laughing helplessly and
reaching for the tissues to wipe our eyes.

"Unbelievable," said Barbara. Probably the one word we
were all thinking.

Brady shook his head. "I'm not sure where we should start.
But we definitely have to use it all. What a circus."

"OK," I replied, "Here's what we'll do. In any existing story,
we can add a paragraph with an update from today. For example, Olivia, have you got something going on the new date for
the candidate selection?"

"Yes. I get what you're saying. I can now add in a paragraph
with your info."

"Great. I'll write up an article on the event as a whole. Then
I'll do a second story for the editorial page called Questions
Raised. And a short one called Bylaw Officer Fired. Brady, I'll
airdrop the pictures and videos to you, if you can organize that
and send a few to Barbara. The rest we'll use on the website."

"For sure. And I'll get a few still photos out of the video as
well."

I glanced over at the whiteboard. "The interesting thing is
that most of what people said or did at the reception ties in
nicely with our list here. Before I start writing, I'll make a few
notes on the board. But don't worry. That'll be for next week. We
have less than 24 hours to get everything we just talked about

over to Barbara, on top of your other stories. It's going to be a rush, so let's get busy."

I stood up and looked at the list. Written in red marker were the names: Councilor Leona Rigg, Sonny Rigg, Jordan Phipps, and Tyler Aston.

I erased 'Bylaw Officer' and wrote Carlton Miner. I then added: Boathouse couple, Dog complaint ladies, Conservative candidates, Moose Logan, and Councilor Cowboy Whitmore.

I think his real name was Charles, but no one ever called him that. The nickname was ironic. He was a high school science teacher who also kept mini-horses on a 50-acre lot just north of town. But people didn't laugh too hard, because as it turned out there was a decent market for mini-horses.

Of course, a lot of our ideas were conjecture based on the idea that Fred Phipps was the mastermind behind some sort of chicanery to do with bylaw enforcement. I wasn't at all sure that that was the case, but at least each interview would make a good story. And the Carlton Miner firing itself would for sure need a follow-up article.

I stopped. Something didn't seem logical. "Olivia, why is it that one person is doing both the bylaw enforcement and building inspection? I thought that it was two separate roles."

She nodded, "It is. But the regular building inspector is on maternity leave. The council thought it would be easier to have one person do both. Carlton's an older man and, in the past, he was the building inspector. It's a pretty complex process, and they don't have anyone else cross-trained. And they didn't want to hire anyone short term."

Brady observed, "That sure gives him a lot of control. Both roles have the potential to impact people's livelihoods."

"I agree," I said. "Some of the bylaws, say, parking or skate-boarding for example, are more of a minor annoyance for people who get caught. But it's different when it comes to property use and that sort of thing."

Next, I took a blue marker and wrote notes after each name, based on things we had heard and the events of the morning.

Standing back and studying it, I frowned. I began to think that all the bylaw nonsense was distracting me from something more important. I mean, people complained about a bylaw officer all the time even if they were doing an honest job. It sort of went with the territory. And I was pretty sure that Reg Johanson was going to live to regret his outburst from this morning.

But the one action that seemed really out of character was that of Tyler Aston. His girlfriend has just had her father murdered, she's clearly distraught. The church hall is filled with local dignitaries and grieving friends of Fred Phipps. And what does Tyler do? When he thinks no one's looking, he pours a healthy amount of hard liquor into an innocuous pink fruit punch.

On the surface, Tyler had a good reputation. Other than for Olivia's local-girl intel, I had never heard a negative thing about him. He was about six feet tall and attractive, with hair as dark as Jordan's and matching brown eyes. Over the years I'd photographed him many times for the paper. Mostly sports teams, but also the occasional club or youth group event. For years he'd left his hair a bit long and he wore it pushed back off his face.

Hair. That brought to mind my own. I still more or less liked how it looked, but I was getting tired of the upkeep. Today was a good example. I'd had to get up early to wash and style it, it had gotten quite wet coming and going this morning, and now it was still hanging all over me, a little on the damp side. I felt like I was working up to a big change. I dragged my thoughts back to business.

OK, Tyler. His family also seemed normal. His father was well-known in town as a family doctor and his mother worked as his medical receptionist. He had a couple of older siblings who had moved on to careers in business and lived somewhere in southern Ontario. As Marley had said, Tyler was going to law school, but still spent a lot of time in Williamsport.

However, I now had some serious questions. We'd already wondered if he was selling drugs and the mayor had found out. I had no clue, and no idea about how to follow this up. Jordan managed a chain restaurant called Mitzi's. It had a retro vibe and Barbara liked it. Maybe I could ask her about the happy couple? Tomorrow, once we got the current issue of the paper off to the printer.

I couldn't stop thinking of the funeral. Tyler had acted on his own. Jordan had not been at his side, there had been no whispers or laughs between the two of them. None of the young men who had attended were around, or watching, or even taking extra glasses. It sure seemed like Tyler was flying solo.

Was it foolish immaturity? Was it malicious? Had he been trying to wind everyone up, and succeeded beyond his wildest dreams?

If he had been looking to draw the attention of the police and general public to a wide range of suspects? Wow, gold star.

Next, I would try to come up with a motive for Tyler Aston. I needed Brady and Olivia for this. So, it would have to wait until Wednesday.

16

Tuesday was a long day but we made it. The paper eventually got to the printer, and first thing Wednesday morning bundles containing fresh copies of the Williamsport Whistle were delivered to sales outlets around town.

There had been a steady stream of people in to chat with me in the seating area in our front office. Most of them were plying me for even more information. Little did they know I was an expert at the same thing. But other than a number of truly hilarious observations and comments, I didn't pick up anything useful.

Once it quieted down, I headed back to the meeting room. Marley was going to be late opening her own office. I'd let her into the back, and she was sitting at the big table with Rocco on her lap. She was feeding him bits of her croissant and drinking a latte.

Out the window, the sun was shining, my gate was being repaired, and the lawn looked like it was starting to sprout. Barbara and Jeff had done a great job at removing the evidence of the fire and launching the process of rejuvenating the yard.

Marley raised her cup, "Cheers! This one is worth framing." She had the front page open on the table and it really was superb. If I did say so. The large headline read 'Memorable Sendoff For Beloved Mayor.' The front page had articles by all three of us, and Brady had done a stellar job on the photos.

"I hope next week's is just as good."

She looked over her shoulder at the whiteboard. "Looks like you have your work cut out for you. Too bad I'm an accountant and not a lawyer, so I could help out when half these people sue you."

"Nobody's going to be suing us. We're going to interview people and write down what they say. I have a lot of witnesses, dozens of photos and some videos. At the very least, they can say 'No comment.' But thanks for the offer."

The bear bells jangled, and I heard Barbara greeting the police chief. Before Arni could make his way down the hall, I had hopped up and written 'Story Ideas' at the top of our suspect list.

Arni looked like it had been a while since he had last had a good night's sleep. His straight blond hair had lost its luster and he had large circles under his eyes. His long-sleeved, pale-yellow shirt was rumpled, and his tie was loosened. He had a stainless-steel, thermal coffee mug and was sipping on it like an addict.

Before he could speak, Olivia came in and took a seat. Brady was only a few seconds behind her. We all gazed at Arni expectantly.

He rolled his eyes and grumbled, "Don't look at me like that."

I said, "You should be flattered. Obviously, we all thought you'd come to tell us you've cracked the case."

"I wish," he said. "Good job with the paper. It must have been hard to restrain yourself."

"The facts spoke for themselves," I replied with a straight face.

"I thought you were going to say 'one picture is worth a thousand words," he said. "I think my favorite was Moose, his tie flying and his eyes bulging." He shook his head, "I have never in my life experienced a scene like that, and don't quote me. I'm very tired."

Olivia asked, "Will there be any charges? According to Zora, there were plenty of assaults."

He sighed, "Probably not. I'll let you know if that changes."

Arni then looked idly at the Story Idea list. "You forgot Ollie Hanson," he said.

"Nope," I said. "We cleared him." I hoped Arni didn't catch my law enforcement terminology. They all looked at me curiously. I thought everyone could use another laugh and so I told them about my weekend adventures. Every time I said the word 'bear' Rocco growled, and Marley gave him a treat. I had to start spelling it.

"Anyway, if he didn't own a gun, even to defend himself from a b-e-a-r, I don't think he'd be likely to shoot Fred. Also, now that I think about it, if he'd really wanted to, he could have looked after the matter without leaving home. No need for him to drive into town and sneak around the Legion."

They all nodded in agreement. Arni frowned. "What does that mean, 'Tyler vodka'?"

Olivia said, "You didn't know?"

"Know what?"

"Zora and I were among the last to arrive in the church hall. We were just standing there, looking around, and we saw Tyler Aston dump a container of vodka into the fruit punch."

Brady said, "I don't know the guy, but he seems a little old for that sort of thing. I could see Sonny Rigg, for example."

Arni rubbed his face with both hands. "I have to go before I say something I shouldn't. Please be careful. This isn't a game. I'm not saying you can't work on your quote/unquote story list. But leave the crime-fighting to trained investigators."

He stood up to go and Marley followed suit. She set the dog down, and he wandered over to his sunny bed.

Once we had the place to ourselves, I looked over at the reporters and said, "I'm a little disappointed. Arni read the whole list and didn't react. I think that means the police aren't seriously looking at any of these people. They must have someone else in mind. I can't even take a guess."

Olivia said, "I don't think it matters. It's still a good story list, and all of these people were at the Legion that night. The one advantage the police have is following up on the handgun, I guess."

Brady added, "You know when we were talking about means, motive, and opportunity? I think we're on the right track. All our people had the opportunity, and I think it's productive to get more information on motive. Who knows? If we go around and interview them, we may get a clearer connection between some of these folks and the mayor."

"I agree," I said. "I'm going to talk to Moose later today. Let's divide up the rest."

By the end of the meeting, it was settled. I would talk to Moose Logan, and the two councilors, Rigg and Whitmore. Olivia would continue her ongoing story about the Conservative party hopefuls and reach out to Tyler and Sonny. We handed the big bylaw officer mess to Brady.

Our first goal would be to get comments on the many allegations made at the funeral. If we could get them talking about Fred Phipps, bonus.

Before I got a start on my interviews, I had something to take care of. There were two high-end hair salons downtown. I'd made my decision. Whichever of the shops had a vacancy this morning would get my business. I'd been trimming my long hair myself for years. Although once in a while I splurged and went to a salon in Toronto. But no more.

I wanted a good short cut, à la Annie Lennox. I knew I was showing my age, and that the young stylists in town probably wouldn't even know who I was talking about, but between Annie and Judi Dench and maybe Rihanna, I hoped they would get the drift.

Celebrities aside, I had to admit that Rocco and I had spent hours last night googling 'women short gray hair' and other similar terms. Of course, I planned to scour the salon magazines before sitting down for the momentous event. But if I didn't see anything, I had about two dozen pictures on my phone to inspire the stylist.

I sent Roc upstairs with a biscuit to put in a shift of guarding and headed out.

17

By the time lunchtime rolled around I was so nervous, I didn't think I could eat a bite. I'd been sitting here in the stylist's chair for so long I was losing track of my original motivation and feeling sick at the thought of what was going on.

Between the two of us, we'd decided on the shape and style of the cut, and that she would also freshen up the color on the remaining hair on the top of my head. If there was any left. I told her I wanted to keep my eyes closed for the duration. I was that nervous.

Midway through the process, I'd peeked at the floor and it was covered in long white hanks of hair. It looked like someone had done a makeover on a bunch of Cowboy Whitmore's ponies, leaving remnants of their manes and tails beside me. My stomach turned over.

I already felt an unfamiliar cold draft on my neck, and the smells of the hair-dye potions were making me nauseated. What had I done?

I'd thought the new look would make me look youthful,

strong, and uncompromising, but what if it was Samson and Delilah all over again? What if I looked scrawny and, well, old?

The stylist was named Valerie, and although I knew she was the owner of the shop, and had years of experience, I was still deathly afraid of what I'd asked her to do. On the upside, she knew who Annie Lennox was. And her own hair always looked spectacular.

"Zora," she asked, "Do you have any makeup with you?"

"Yes," I replied. "It's in a small bag in my purse. Go ahead."

"Great. Keep your eyes closed. I want to update your look."

I didn't know I had a look.

Valerie began swiping away at my eyes, face, and lips. It took much longer than I expected. But finally, she turned the chair back towards the mirror and said, "Zora. It's time. You're ready."

I opened my eyes and hardly recognized the person looking back at me. Tears came to my eyes as everyone in the shop, hairdressers and customers alike, gathered around and clapped and cheered. My new hair was super short up the sides with a bright, white tousled cap on top. Or as Valerie said, 'tussled.' That's ok. She was a genius haircutter. I wouldn't quibble with her grammar.

My eyes looked larger and bluer, and my cheekbones and jawline looked sharper. Valerie was rambling on about how I could also wear the hair spiky or smoothed down in bangs. She brought over an array of product, and I said 'yes' to everything.

"Valerie, I cannot believe it. It's exactly how I hoped it would turn out," I exclaimed. I swear I saw her heave a visible sigh of relief. "Thank you so much."

It took a while to get out of the salon. Who knew that a radical haircut was a path to celebrity? But eventually, I paid my bill and headed up to Marley's office. It felt surreal. I really did feel lighter. Now I knew why Rocco always went wild, running and jumping after getting groomed. It was a totally giddy feeling. The warm breeze blew on my face and I had to stop myself from the habit of pushing my hair back. Seeing as it wasn't there anymore. What an amazing sensation.

Marley was with a client, but I waved at her through her office window. She did a classic double-take, rushed out to hug me, and ruffled her hands over the buzzed part of my new do. I swear it was the same routine she went through with Rocco.

We were both laughing by this point. "I can't believe you did it!" she said. "Congratulations. You look about 25."

"Thank you very much." I knew it wasn't true, but it was nice of her to say so. "Back to work. For both of us. Talk to you later."

I skipped going into my office and instead headed down the lane to get my car. As long as I was still feeling so confident, I wanted to corner Moose Logan at The Penalty Box. And I also felt guilty about taking the morning off.

My appetite was returning, and I had a craving for spinach salad and an iced tea. I decided to get myself served before interviewing Moose, in case he got mad. Who was I kidding? I wanted to eat before he for sure freaked out, yelled at me, and threw me out of his restaurant.

In less than 10 minutes, I was seated at the bar trying to get used to the attention my new look was garnering. Moose said, "Turn around." I obeyed. He shook his head and said, "You need to go back."

"What? Why?" I asked.

"You need to get them to buzz a 'Z' into the back. What a missed opportunity."

"One step at a time. By the way, may I please order?"

I waited until I had finished most of my meal, and by then the noon-hour crowd had dispersed and the restaurant was mostly empty.

Moose headed over my way to wipe down the bar and I got my nerve up. "So, can I ask you something?"

He replied, "You know, I'll be polite to you in public and you and your friends can come in here like usual. But I don't see why I should do you any favors. Not after you put my picture in the paper."

"A lot of people got their picture in the paper."

"That's true." He let that hang there. I was puzzled.

"Anyway, you have to admit that losing your cool at a man's funeral is a way to get attention."

He shrugged. And so far, he didn't look angry, so I continued. "A lot of things were said yesterday morning. Not to mention Carlton Miner getting fired. You can't be surprised that the local newspaper would follow up."

"It was all bull," he said, his voice a little louder. "I don't see what the big deal is anyway. Once I lock the doors, it's my property. If my friends happen to be in here with me, that's my business."

"I heard that the mayor came out here to talk to you and you lost it, yelled at him, and called him a fascist."

"Maybe."

"Moose, I'm not trying to do some smear story about you or your business. What I really want to know is what happened that day with the mayor. How were things left?"

I thought this could go one of two ways. If Fred Phipps had retreated, it would mean he had gone through the motions, made it look like he was taking action on someone bending the rules. But in fact, sending a message to the bar owner that it was business as usual.

But if Fred had left Moose with a threat of charges, I'd take that to mean the mayor was honest. Despite Moose's blustering, he well knew he was breaking the law by serving alcohol after 2:00 a.m. If charges still had not been laid, that would indicate that the problem lay with Carlton Miner or whoever was pulling his strings.

It would also give Moose a motive for the killing.

I was a little annoyed at myself. No sooner had I thought of this than I began playing devil's advocate. For Moose, of all people. Would such a hot-headed guy be the type to organize a shooting in a public place? Make his escape? Not betray himself with his expressions or actions? Not likely.

Anyway, I soon got my answer. "Why do you think I got so mad? He said that the next time anyone complained, he was sending over the bylaw officer to charge me and calling the liquor board as well."

I was extra pleased that this interview had been conducted without any shouting or objects being thrown. I took a last sip of my iced tea and paid my bill.

As I turned to go, Moose added, "By the way, Zora, I didn't kill him."

I more or less believed him.

18

I was sitting in my office, laptop open, putting together my notes from my chat with Moose Logan. Next, I planned to set up appointments to meet with Councilors Rigg and Whitmore.

Barbara had gone wild about my new look. She said she loved it and that it made me look like the 'cat's meow.' Now she was up front humming 'Santa Baby.' This was her go-to tune when she was concentrating. In all four seasons.

I'd already had texts from the reporters asking me about my hair, so I knew the town grapevine was working. Little did I know exactly how well.

I heard the front door open and was a little surprised to hear the police chief's voice again. This time, I got up out of my seat and went to the reception area. "Hi Arni, what can we do for you?"

This time there were no smiles. He still looked exhausted, but he was all business. "Zora, I need you to accompany me to the station."

My jaw must have dropped, and Barbara looked stricken.

He followed me while I went and got my purse and phone and we went out to his car. "Do I have to sit in the back?" I asked.

"Not today," was the reply. Not exactly reassuring.

Once we got to the police station, I was seated in an interview room. Arni came in and he was joined by Constable Renée Winters.

The constable had a stocky build and gave off a pit bull vibe. She had straight, dark brown hair that was scraped back into a tight ponytail, a style that did nothing to flatter her round face. Her small brown eyes looked at me accusingly.

I had to give her credit for the rest of her appearance, though. Renee was the ultimate professional. Her fitted navy blue shirt and uniform pants were crisp and immaculate. For all I knew she lounged around in ratty sweatpants and bunny slippers at home, but somehow I doubted it.

Renée and I had never really hit it off. To put it mildly. I think she had a crush on Arni and was jealous of our easygoing relationship. I couldn't think of anything else I had done to annoy her. She was the one who had given me the speeding ticket, after all. Anyway, she sat across the table from me and took notes. Living up to her surname. There was a real chill in the air. Thank goodness it was the chief asking the questions.

"Zora, it doesn't seem right that I don't have much of a statement from you, given that you were the one to find the mayor."

Renée shot him a glance.

"Not only did you find the body, but you were in the room when he was attacked. I can't not bring you in."

This sounded like the court of public opinion had spoken and was exacting revenge. "Let me guess," I said. "After people got their hands on today's paper, you started getting anonymous tips."

"It doesn't matter whether or not they were anonymous. They were tips and we have to follow up. Now, first, can you please go over everything that happened last Thursday night at the Legion."

I did. I'm not saying I enjoyed it, but it was pretty straightforward. And not something that was likely to fade from memory.

"What was your relationship with the mayor? At the funeral, Jordan stated that he didn't really like you."

"It was fine. I didn't know him all that well. All three of us covered council meetings on occasion and, with Fred having a pretty peaceful tenure in office, I can't say that we ever got into any conflict."

"Thank you. Now, were you in Toronto at any time in the last two months?"

What was this all about? "Yes, probably. I'd have to check. But I think I went shopping just after Easter."

"Were you by yourself? Can anyone corroborate any of your activities?"

"Rocco was with me."

"Other than the dog."

"No." There it was. My first lie to the police. But I wasn't going to give up my secret relationship with Darius. I guess if I were ever under oath, I'd tell the truth. But not yet. If it came to it, I was pretty sure between our two credit cards we could trace the path we'd taken from stores to restaurants to clubs over the course of the weekend.

"Have you ever attended the Gun Club?"

"Of course not."

I was beginning to get a bit worried. If Arni thought I'd gone out of town to purchase a gun, and various people were willing to swear that I could shoot one, this might get serious.

"You were seen back at the Legion on Friday. Can you please state for the record what you were doing?"

"Oh, you mean retrieving the murder weapon?" They both looked up at me sharply. "For heaven's sake. I'm joking. I went over there on Friday afternoon with the reporters so they could see the scene, since I knew we'd all be writing about it for days. All the media were there, not just us."

"Did you enter either of the restrooms at any time on Friday?"

"That would be no. Seeing as you had officers posted there the whole time. Now, are we just about finished here?"

He nodded, and I got up and left. I had no car and it was quite a hike back downtown but, after that interrogation, I sure felt like a walk.

I had put on a brave front and tried to appear calm and as tough as my new image might imply. But this could become a disaster if they didn't catch the killer soon. I thought back to Moose's response when I had noted 'a lot of people' had their pictures in the paper. If everyone who ever took offense at a photo or article banded together and left anonymous messages with the police, my business would suffer.

The fact that Arni had picked me up for questioning made me feel like a web of lies and innuendo was closing in. If advertisers believed that I was guilty, and only avoiding arrest due to my so-called friendship with the police chief, it would have a swift impact. I was already worried about the employees. They all depended on the salary I paid them.

I picked up the pace of my walking. I was glad I had on comfortable black leather ankle boots. I took a moment to savor the fresh air blowing in my face and feel the sun. So different than with long hair. But the novelty was not enough to ward off my worst fears. What if I was arrested? The paper could never survive the prolonged absence of any one of us. Staffing and finances were just too tight in this day and age. I walked even faster.

Soon enough I was trotting in the front door, ready to get busy. If the police were reduced to questioning me, they were miles away from catching the murderer. I stopped in my tracks. Barbara was the cheeriest and most even-tempered person I knew. But she was sitting at her desk with red eyes and the minute she saw me, tears flowed down her cheeks. She dabbed at her nose with a tissue.

"What in the world is the matter?" I said rushing over to her.

"I didn't want to tell you. Now I don't know what to do," she was sobbing in earnest now.

"Barbara, I can't help if you don't explain."

Silently she pulled a plastic Bulk Barn bag out of her desk drawer and handed it to me. It was quite heavy, and I had no idea what was inside. Probably not rice or lentils. Or chocolate-covered almonds.

I peeked inside and almost dropped the thing. It was covered in mud, charred grass and black cinders and what looked like part of one of my shirts. But there was no mistaking the object. It was a handgun. The first one I had ever seen, not counting TV and movies.

To say I was shocked didn't come close.

I was not one for stuttering, but I heard my own voice, "H... how? W... where?"

Barbara wiped her eyes and pushed the button on her speakers to turn off Frank Sinatra. "When Jeff and I were cleaning up the yard last night I found it while I was raking. I hid it right away. Jeff doesn't even know."

I said with a calm I did not feel, "Barbara, call Arni right now and get him over here. You have to tell him exactly what you told me. I know it looks bad, but I think it just means that the killer was the same person who set the fire, just as we thought. I highly doubt I would have tossed the weapon in my own yard if I had just killed someone."

She brightened up. I could only hope that Arni agreed. She picked up the office phone and began to talk. It wasn't closing time yet, but I locked the door and flipped the sign asking people to come back tomorrow morning at 8:30. Then I changed my mind. I went next door and ordered a large latte, returned to my office, and waited. I tried to let the savory, calming beverage work its magic but it was tough going.

19

It wasn't long before Arni was at the door, and I told Barbara to take him back to the meeting room.

I could hear them talking in an undertone, but I sat out front at her desk in case we had any visitors. And I sincerely hoped we did not. As I expected, it was only a few minutes until Barbara returned. She whispered, "Sorry. He wants to talk to you now."

"You did the right thing. Don't apologize."

I went and sat down opposite Arni. He was all business, and said, "Have you ever seen this gun before?"

I stopped myself from rolling my eyes and said, "No. I've never seen it. And I don't own any firearms."

He then had me go over my statement from the night of the fire. We even went out onto the back deck and then upstairs to my apartment balcony so he could verify the lines of sight I was trying to describe. Because my privacy fence was so high, it was impossible to see anything in the laneway from downstairs, and very little from upstairs. Again, I bit my tongue. That was the whole point of the fence.

The person who had thrown the Molotov cocktails had only

caught my attention with a flash of light. Not because I had seen them. And only then because Rocco had been barking.

The seriousness of the situation was broken up by my pet's antics. He threw his orange ball at Arni. He threw his kong at Arni. Getting no response, he batted the ball under the sofa and then crouched and barked at it because it was out of reach. Loudly.

To distract him, I let him go downstairs with me. He made a beeline for Barbara, and she looked very happy to have a fuzzy beige poodle to cuddle.

Arni and I returned to the meeting room, and I said bluntly, "I need to know how your investigation is going. I can assure you I did not murder the mayor or burn up all my clothes. You have to catch this person before my business is destroyed. I have no idea who is leaving you anonymous tips, but if you look in this week's paper, you'll probably see their pictures."

I didn't say anything out loud but I reflected that, for too long, I'd sort of had a cavalier attitude about running the paper. Week after week, reporting on all and sundry, plastering their photos around online and in print. I certainly prided myself on being sensitive to the values of a small town, and I considered each article carefully before it was published. But it seemed like the tables had turned. Someone was using the crisis of the unsolved murder to slander me in a way I had never even contemplated doing in the newspaper.

Arni stood up without answering. "I'll be in touch," he said.

I followed him towards the front door and paused as Olivia passed him on the way in. Holding the door for her was Tyler Aston. He nodded at Arni and sauntered into the reception area. He was dressed casually in khaki board shorts and a short-sleeved red t-shirt branded by a running shoe company. The same company had made his flip-flops.

Olivia said, "Hi Zora. I just met Tyler on the street and

mentioned that I wanted to talk to him. He said he had time to chat now."

"Be my guest," I replied, and they headed back to the meeting room. I waited a discreet amount of time and then went and sat in my office. This place was far from soundproof, and since Tyler was at the top of my suspect list today, I couldn't resist listening in. I was curious about whether Olivia's interview would give me any insight as to motive.

Olivia said, "Tyler, thanks so much for coming in. We're still doing a lot of follow-up interviews. So many people were affected by Mayor Phipps' death." I knew she wouldn't have any trouble looking sorrowful.

Tyler replied, "Yes. Jordan is devastated. I know he was a public figure and everything, but he was her father."

"Were they close?"

"For sure. You probably know she still lived at home. It's a big place out in the country, and I think they were company for each other. She works long hours, and it's not like she spends a lot of time in town partying. It works out well for both of them. I guess I should say 'worked.'"

Hmm. Mr. Sensitivity. He was hitting all the right notes so far.

"Tyler, you and Jordan must have talked about this. Do either of you have any idea about who could possibly have killed the mayor?"

"I know she was rambling at the reception about a girlfriend. But I never heard anything about that. I got along well with Fred, and he never confided in me, either. Personally, I think it must have had something to do with politics."

I wished that I could see his face. There was a funny tone in his voice. Did he really know something?

"Can I check a rumor with you? You might be upset."

"It's fine. Go ahead."

"Um, OK. Well, someone told us that you spiked the punch at the funeral."

Silence.

"Busted. Yeah, I put some vodka in it."

"Can I ask why? It was a little early in the day."

"Can this be off the record? I don't want Jordan to know anything about this."

"Sure. It's a longer story and I don't have to include every word you say."

"Well, between you and me I have a pretty good idea about who killed Fred. I was hoping if he got drunk in public, he might give himself away."

I sat up straighter. This was news. It sounded like law-student Tyler had been reading too much John Grisham. I hated to admit it, but Arni was right. Tyler was a kid. He should take his suspicions to the police and not run around playing detective. He could even telephone anonymously, if he could ever get through. With all those people calling to lie about me, he might have to try a few times before the line was free.

Olivia followed up with, "Wow, Tyler, that's a bit of a bombshell. Maybe you should let us include your comment. That might shake them up. You could even tell me who you think it was. You know I couldn't print it without proof." Olivia wasn't much of a giggler, but she added a fake laugh at this point.

There was a pause, and then he said, "I'm not naming any names. But, sure, go ahead."

"Tyler, I appreciate that. But I'm having second thoughts. I'd feel terrible if anything happened to you because of something I wrote in the paper. Maybe instead of telling me anything more, you should speak to the police."

"Nah, they won't do anything. These kinds of people? They always get their own way. And I'm not afraid of the old fart anyway."

"Maybe you should be. We're talking about someone who has already killed once. Plus tried to burn this building down."

"You know what? He should be more afraid of me."

This did not give me a good feeling. Tyler was over-confident. What had he just revealed to Olivia? The person he suspected was older, powerful, male, and comfortable with guns. Tyler was sitting on a powder keg. I thought I should probably intervene.

But I still hesitated. And not for business reasons. There was no way we were going to print most of what Jordan's boyfriend had just told Olivia. But I didn't want to undercut her as the interviewer. I stayed put.

Besides, there was nothing anyone could do. Even if Tyler told Arni exactly what he'd just told us, he would still be sent home with the advice to be careful.

I waited a few more minutes until I heard Tyler walk past my door. Then I couldn't restrain myself. I followed him out onto the sidewalk and said, "Thanks for sitting down with Olivia."

He looked at me like I was crazy, but said, "No problem."

"I couldn't forgive myself if I didn't come after you. All of this is so unlike our little town. I'm asking you seriously to take your suspicions to the police."

He gazed past me and didn't meet my eye. "I'll think about it," he muttered.

I headed back inside.

Finally, this day was over. I shooed the others out of the office, beckoned to Rocco, and went upstairs. I collapsed on the couch and just tried to relax for half an hour before making dinner.

Then I waited until it was almost dark. For too long lately, Rocco and I had skipped our routine. I put on my running shoes, clipped the leash on him, and we went for a long, relaxing walk along the nighttime streets.

20

I felt like I was chained to my washer and dryer. With so few clothes, I had to wash and dry every day or two. Here it was, 7:00 a.m., and I was at it again. I gave up on my austerity measure. I texted Marley to see if she had time to take a long lunch and advise me on some new purchases. I expected a 'yes,' and I was not disappointed. We agreed to meet at noon.

I looked into my bedroom and there was no sign of Rocco. He'd taken advantage of my absence to crawl under the sheets. More laundry. He snapped at me on the way by, as I shooed him out of the room and added the linens to the load. This was another one of his charming behaviors, air-snaps. He'd never actually bite, but he liked to look tough at all times.

Before I could return to the kitchen, I heard a rhythmic metallic clanging. The Prince was at it again. He must have eaten all his dog food during the night and left the bowl empty. An unacceptable state of affairs. He would smack the bowl until it was filled, so I went and shook some kibble into it right away. He gave a sniff as if to verify the contents and walked away. He wasn't hungry. He just didn't like to see an empty bowl.

I missed being able to put the dog out into the backyard. The new grass seed was sprouting, covering the yard with feathery, pale green tufts, and I didn't want to mess up the work done by Barbara and Jeff. I put on my exercise clothes and runners and walked Rocco around the block. I couldn't help thinking of the women who had challenged Carlton Miner at the funeral and took a good supply of plastic bags with me.

First on the agenda, once I arrived at work, was an editorial meeting. It was time to compare notes on our articles and decide on a list for next week's edition. And I felt we needed to get a handle on all the stories that were not related to Fred Phipps.

While I waited for Brady and Olivia to arrive, I looked through the various media releases, hand-written notes, and telephone messages that had been left in the past few days.

For some events, we would do short advance articles, and we always tried to fit in as many pictures of special occasions as possible. Brady wrote up the police notices and this went much faster than in the past. We used to have to call the station to get information on recent incidents before each weekly deadline. Now, the police department was using social media, and it was pretty straightforward to use this information for our own website and Instagram account. Olivia stayed in touch with the schools and they were always busy with creative programs and sports events. Not to mention cute, photogenic children.

As well, we always got a few photos submitted from readers every week. They were usually winners and this week was no exception. We had received a blurry digital photo of a raccoon behind the steering wheel of a guy's Jeep. I hoped Brady could clean it up so we could use it.

As well, there was a lovely photo of a smiling 90-year-old woman on her milestone birthday. Unfortunately, she was seated in a wheelchair in front of a floral arrangement that made her look like she was wearing a large rack of deer antlers. Another job for Brady.

Once we were all seated around the meeting room table, I said, "Thanks for all your hard work on the aftermath of Fred Phipps' death. Let's recap what we have so far."

Since I had eavesdropped on Olivia's interview, there were no surprises there.

Brady said, "I managed to track down some of the people who were complaining about the bylaw officer. I got statements from the women regarding Whitmore's dog and his ... visitations. And I got more than an earful from those boathouse people. But Carlton Miner won't talk to me."

I replied, "This may be a good time for me to say this. I will follow up with Carlton Miner. I will also follow up with all the politicians. We still have a paper to put out, and there are a lot of other stories to research and write."

Olivia said, "I'm supposed to speak to Sonny Rigg this afternoon."

"That should be fine. But I want to explain. I'm concerned on a number of counts. One. The murderer has not been caught. Two. We don't know who torched my yard. Three. Tyler Aston thinks he's a character out of a movie and is invincible. Four. People are calling the police anonymously and accusing me of being involved."

The reporters nodded soberly.

"Now, on that last point. I can't stress how serious this is. If the rumors affect advertising, it will have an immediate impact on our ability to continue with the present business model."

The reporters looked at each other. Brady said, "We have to get this sorted out. I need my job."

"Same," said Olivia.

"The sorting out will be done by me. I don't want either of

you in the line of fire. And I'm not speaking metaphorically here. I'm determined to get to the bottom of this, and I also want you to be safe."

We carried on for another half hour, making up a list of stories and assignments.

I knew I had a crazy amount of work facing me. But it wouldn't get done if I had no clothing to wear, I reasoned. It was time to shop.

I called Marley and we agreed to take my car. When I pulled up in front of her office, she hopped in right away. I didn't think I was stopped long enough for it even to be counted as double parking. We planned to canvas the mall, the various stores at the new suburban plaza, and then finish up with the main street shops. And lunch.

It was a whirlwind expedition but was made easier because all I wanted was tights and tops. By the time we were finished, I was the proud new owner of a solid seven days' worth of clothing. I also broke down and bought a bunch of new underwear at Walmart. I hoped to now be able to give the washer a much-deserved rest.

Although Rocco would be disappointed. The machine played eight bars of tinkly, nursery-rhyme music when it finished a wash cycle, and Roc leaped up and ran to find his orange ball every time he heard the tune. He'd even go through the same routine if I sang it for him.

His motivation was simple. If I were standing on the deck hanging clothes, he could drop the ball at my feet and bark, and I'd throw it across the lawn for him. His whole routine had been disrupted by the arsonist. It wasn't the same, when all I had to do was toss the wet clothes into the dryer.

Marley and I chose one of our favorite cafés for a quick lunch. It had the front patio doors open to the street and we had a ringside seat. It was summery and hot, and the biting spring insects that patrolled the countryside in June were non-existent here on the main street of Williamsport. Traffic was light, and a few young mothers strolled by with their babies. The last of the lunch bunch from the high school went by, a dozen teenagers horsing around and eating slices of pizza.

Marley said, "That was a blast. I really like all your new stuff. And I may have to go back to a few stores myself and try some things on."

"Thanks for all your advice. I still miss my old favorites, but it will be fun to mix and match some new combinations. I have to say it might be a while before I feel like hanging my clothes out to dry again." Washer song or no washer song.

We ordered the soup and salad special with iced tea to drink, and people-watched as we waited. Just as the server brought our order, a kid zoomed right by us on a fancy skateboard.

Marley said, "Where's Carlton Miner when you need him? I thought that kid was going to take a sip of my tea on the way by."

"I guess they'll have to replace Carlton. But I still think he has a chance at getting his job back. I mean he's a municipal worker. There must be some sort of formal process involved. You don't just blow your stack in public and can town employees."

The skateboarder had the balance and coordination of an Olympic gymnast. In one fluid motion, he hopped off and, on the way, flipped the board up so he could catch it as he waited for the red light at the intersection to turn green.

To my surprise, before the light could change, none other than Carlton Miner jogged up beside him. He was in his full bylaw officer regalia of smart gray shirt and black slacks, and had his citation book in hand.

Marley and I looked at each other and burst out laughing. We sipped our soups and ate spears of salad while we waited for

Carlton to finish writing the young man a ticket for skate-boarding on the sidewalk.

"Yoo hoo, Carlton," I called. Marley waved him over to our seat in the window, and I quickly went outside to join him on the sidewalk.

"Hi. I just wanted to say I'm glad you're back." What I was really glad about was the chance to ask him a few questions without taking the time to track him down. I thought it was very cooperative of him to show up at my lunch table.

At first, he had frowned at the sight of me, but my remarks warmed him up a bit and he didn't walk away. Yet. Marley did me a favor and asked him, "So, all I heard was what happened at the funeral. But I didn't think they could make that stick."

He agreed. "It's hard working for the fire chief. We've never liked each other since we were kids. Then he married my cousin's sister-in-law, and I have to see him at family things." My head was spinning. I wanted to know if he had killed the mayor, not write a genealogy report.

"Carlton, all the things that people were saying. Is there any truth to them? Was the mayor or someone on council giving you instructions about how to do your job?"

He hesitated just a second too long before answering, "Oh, no. You know what it's like in a small town. People are always complaining."

"So, you personally make all the enforcement decisions?"

Now he looked like he wished he had a skateboard himself, so he could get away from me. "Yes, that's correct," he muttered, quickly adding, "I have to be going now. You ladies have a nice day."

I went back inside to finish my Caesar and minestrone. "What did you make of that?" I asked Marley around mouthfuls of romaine lettuce.

"Someone's telling him what to do."

"If I had to take a guess, I'd say it was not the mayor. He looked like he was still feeling the pressure."

"I agree."

"On another topic. We haven't been to Cruise Night yet this year. How about tonight?"

"Fantastic idea. It's the perfect weather for it."

21

Marley and I didn't linger over our meals, even though we were tempted. There was something about the early summer air that was intoxicating. I had to get my car from the parking lot behind the restaurant, and I decided to drive it home and then liberate Rocco for a refreshing, midday stroll. As the boss, I deserved some perks, I told myself.

Roc was more than happy to get out and stretch his legs. He looked cute as usual, prancing along at the end of his royal blue leash. All an illusion as I knew far too well, but he did bring a smile to the faces of passersby. We walked along Main Street, and my interest was piqued. Not by the colorful spring fashions in the shops and boutiques. I'd already had my fill for the day. No, I was excited at the sight of Councilor Leona Rigg just ahead of me.

Her yellow hair shone in the sunlight, and she was wearing stretchy jeans and a short-sleeved blue plaid shirt.

Leona owned a popular shop, which I had just passed. It was called Bear Claw Art and Gifts and it had, by far, the best selection of work by local artisans, painters, and jewelers, along with many craft and gift items.

As I followed her, I could see that she was carrying a lunch tote, and I wondered if she might be headed for the park benches that lined the boardwalk and the town docks. I often walked Rocco in that area and, sure enough, a minute or two later we were headed down the picturesque, cobblestone garden path that led to the waterfront.

I slowed my pace. Rocco didn't mind, as it gave him more time to sniff the large granite boulders and neat annual plants that decorated our path. I saw Leona sit down on one side of a shaded picnic table, setting her lunch bag beside her on the bench. I approached her and said, "Hello, Leona."

She returned my greeting and then sat quietly gazing out over the water. A couple of kayaks floated by and I could hear the rumble of a larger boat engine in the distance. I sat down opposite her and asked, "Is it all right if I join you for a few minutes?" I put the handle of Rocco's leash firmly under my right foot. He would be happy to stop, as the underside of a picnic table could occupy him for a good long time.

"Oh, sure. That's one cute pup you have." The sight of Rocco poking around at her feet seemed to cheer her up, and she gave his head a little scratch.

"It's a difficult time," I said, trying to start a conversation without actually asking her if she'd had any homicidal thoughts lately.

"Yes," she sighed. "I miss Fred a lot. We'd been acquaintances and then council members together for so many years. He was such a strong leader and a positive influence on the group."

That gave me a bit of an opening. "You must have been shocked at the scene at the reception the other day."

"Oh, it was just awful. At a time when we should have been quietly honoring Fred's memory, that ruckus had to break out. All the shouting, and people actually coming to blows. I couldn't believe my eyes."

"There were so many accusations. I'm surprised the police haven't been following up." Well, that was certainly the truth. If they could bring me in for questioning, the least they could do would be to round up the likes of Moose Logan and Carlton Miner.

"I don't know. Maybe people just chose that way to let their feelings out." Leona shook her head. "But really, it was disgraceful."

"Speaking of those characters, I just ran into Carlton Miner."

Leona rolled her eyes. "Another tempest in a teapot. Why the fire chief had to pick that moment to sack the bylaw officer is beyond me. As if."

"Yes, I figured there must be some sort of due process."

She nodded and reached into her lunch-bag for a plastic container of raw vegetables. She offered me my choice of celery or carrot sticks, but I said, "I just treated myself to a salad. I'm fine, thank you."

She continued, "Of course, if the chief, or any other supervisor for that matter, wants to address a problem with an employee, they can. For heaven's sake, we have a huge human resources manual with instructions."

I decided to prompt her a little more obviously. "Still, I have to say my curiosity was aroused. Not one but several complaints were aired that morning. I don't mind sharing with you that the reporters are following up with some of the people who spoke out."

Leona frowned, "Well, I guess you have a job to do. I really think you might have waited a respectable amount of time before starting this type of muck-raking."

"But weren't you curious, yourself?" I knew I was walking on eggshells here. The councilor could easily tell me to go jump in the lake. And it was only a few feet away. OK, it was a river, but a wide one, and I'd get just as wet. "Some of those people were awfully specific. I certainly don't want to think Fred was protecting someone. As a matter of fact, I admired him."

This was met by silence, so I continued. "I'm no detective. But when I spoke to Carlton just now, well, let's just say I have my doubts."

Leona continued to gaze out over the water. Since I was facing her, my view was different, a grassy bank with cedar shrubs and graceful white birch trees. I sincerely hoped no squirrels showed their little faces and bushy tails. It would be more than Rocco could stand.

Finally, she spoke up. "I'm not sure. I personally wouldn't put up with any irregularities. And I'm a hundred percent sure Fred wouldn't have. So I guess I'll have to take a closer look at the rumors. It's so hard to think that someone you've known for ages might be breaking the law. What you're implying is that there's an issue with either another councilor. Or councilors. Or senior staff."

I let her digest her own remarks for a minute. Sure enough, she looked up and met my eyes. "I guess what you're also saying is that whoever is tied up in this mess might also be..."

"Yes," I said. "And I'm not pointing any fingers. I honestly have no idea what's going on. But I do have a vested interest in having this crime solved soon. It's not going to do my business any good if I'm being questioned by the police. Yes, I was there. But as I've said about a million times, I didn't see anything. I have absolutely no idea who is responsible. I wish I did."

Suddenly my eye was caught by a small plastic sandwich bag fluttering around under the picnic table and about to be swept away by the breeze. I quickly reached down, picked it up, and surreptitiously stuffed it in my bag. This was not a good sign.

Fortunately, Leona was again staring out over the water at some boat traffic and a group of tourists enjoying themselves on the restaurant patio on the other side of the river.

I sneaked a look under the table. My worst fears were realized. Rocco had stood up on his hind legs underneath the table and had tipped over Leona's little tote bag. It was lying on the bench with the opening hanging over the inside edge of the bench. That poodle had the claws and teeth of a safecracker. He had a criminal history of lunch thievery and was obviously at it again. With half a sandwich stuffed in his cheeks, he was looking around for a way to escape with it. I swiftly grabbed the leash and held on firmly.

In the past, he had broken into much harder targets. Any time I had a tradesperson in my home I had to warn them, 'Lock your lunch in the bathroom or my bedroom, if you ever want to see it again.' Rocco had tipped over and ransacked a hard-shell lunch box, and also found an open zippered compartment on a durable canvas kit and used it to raid the interior. His plunder had ranged from tuna sandwiches to homemade cake. The last time, he'd scrounged a cheese and pickle sandwich, leaving the guy with just the pickles.

I needed to diplomatically make my exit. With any luck, Leona would think she had absentmindedly left her sandwich at home.

I stood up and said, "Leona, I'll let you get back to your lunch." What was left of it.

She nodded, and said, "You've given me something to think about."

Before I turned away, I said, "If I could give you some advice? Be careful and contact the police if you have any information."

I helped Rocco make his escape. Aiding and abetting. Now there was a charge Arni could make stick.

On the way back to the office, I couldn't help thinking that Leona had sounded sincere. I might be forced to take her off our list.

22

After lunch, I went back to the office, emailed Brady my notes and quotes from Carlton Miner, and made some phone calls.

Then I told Barbara I was going home. As in upstairs. I could think things over just as easily lounging on my own couch as seated downstairs. I had all day tomorrow to contact at least two councilors and the head of the Conservative riding association.

But for now, I would mull things over with a poodle on my lap. I stretched out on the couch with a big squishy cushion behind my head.

Rocco came and sat on my legs, looking out the window at the blue sky and guarding for pigeons. His fur was wavy and a pale champagne color. He had the typical poodle apricot shadings on his ears, and down his back. His most unique feature, among many, was his claws. The front set of toenails was black, and the back claws were white.

Three names were chasing themselves in circles around my brain: Leona Rigg, Cowboy Whitmore, and Jasper Butler, the riding association president.

"What would you do with them, Roc?" I asked.

"Bite them!"

If only it were that straightforward.

I got up and made myself a chicken sandwich for dinner, adding a small kale salad on the side. Nothing too filling. This was intentional, because Cruise Night always involved a follow-up trip to the ice cream shop. The first part of the evening would be spent walking around the Canadian Tire parking lot, looking at beautiful antique cars. I'd never kept track, but it seemed like the vehicles represented all the decades of the past century. It was really fun talking to the owners, and I could never stop myself from taking photos.

Afterward, Marley and I would go cruising ourselves, straight out Highway 60 to the ice cream parlor, and their list of about 100 different types of ice cream. The day they ever stopped serving Muskoka Mocha would be a tragic one. I never got anything else. Creamy mocha ice cream, a rich chocolate fudge ripple, and tiny dark-chocolate 'fish.' Heavenly.

Plus, even though I never changed my order I could live vicariously through my friend. Marley always tried a different flavor, from Moose Tracks to Black Raspberry Thunder to mango sherbet.

We always met at 7:00 p.m. As I approached, I could see that the Canadian Tire parking lot was already full, between shiny show cars and visitors. I parked in the lot next door, in front of the liquor store. I saw Marley pulling in and we were able to walk over together. Rocco loved Cruise Night. He was well-behaved around humans and, hopefully, there wouldn't be too many other dogs. He pranced along at the end of the short blue leash that matched his royal collar. His beige ears were floppy, his bright eyes were keeping an eye on everything, and his super-sniffer black nose was lifted in the breeze.

Almost as soon as we got to the show, we ran into some friends. Marley stopped to chat, and I kept walking. I don't know who was more eager to wander around, me or the dog. In the first row were a 1949 Monarch sedan in a glamorous turquoise and white two-tone, and a regal dark green 1937 DeSoto coach. These two beauties were followed by a powerful-looking cherry-red 1966 Chevy II, and a shiny white '72 Ford Mustang Shelby 350 fastback.

I knew next to nothing about cars, and it was a good job that they all had custom signs and posters in front to identify them. I was fascinated with the colors and designs and enjoyed talking to the enthusiastic car owners who had so lovingly restored their vehicles. Just looking at the cars seemed to bring back the romance of another age.

I stopped to talk to the woman with the Mustang. She said she and her late husband, Mike, had always loved Mustangs, and the restoration of this one had been a retirement project. She was wearing jeans and a Beach Boys t-shirt and had shoulder-length curly red hair, and green eyes that filled with tears as she spoke about Mike. But then she smiled and bent down to pat Rocco. He was always able to cheer someone up. "Oh, look at that," she chuckled. "He has a racing stripe."

I laughed, too. It figured that it would take a car-lover to properly identify the apricot stripe down the center of Roc's back. After a few more minutes of small talk, we carried on.

One of my favorite cars tonight was parked along the back edge of the lot in the shade. I headed towards a '57 Chrysler 300 with sleek, jet-black paint. It had a huge ferocious-looking chrome grill and long swooping tailfins. I stood for a while admiring it and taking pictures.

When the owner finished talking to some other viewers, and turned towards me and smiled, I thought he looked familiar. He was an older man with a few wrinkles and a shaved head, looking pretty cool in large black sunglasses. He was wearing worn black jeans and a new white t-shirt. I said, "Hi," and looked back at the car. The front passenger door was open, and I could see a black leather jacket slung over the back of the seat and a box of CD's on display, with several fanned out so passersby could see them.

Now I knew where I had seen the man. It was Bernie Butler. His band, 'Bernie & The Billytown Bandits,' had provided the musical interlude at the political meeting a week ago. Now it looked like they had just released a CD. I couldn't believe that a whole week had passed since the death of the mayor in the men's room of the Legion.

I looked over at Bernie, comparing him to my recollection of his brother. They were both tall and bald, but Bernie's face was angular while Jasper's was sort of puffy. Bernie looked happier and was obviously proud of the work he'd done on the car.

Whoops! Before I could stop him, Rocco had jumped into the front seat and was poking around in the footwell. "Hey, you," I said. "Out!"

Bernie was good-natured about the whole thing. Thankfully the dog had not jumped up on the upholstery or anything. He said, "That's OK. I try to drive Bertha around as much as I can. People often sit up front with me. I'm sure he put less dirt in there than my buddies."

I noticed that Bernie was very fond of words starting with the letter 'B'. Maybe all those years of having an alliterative name had affected his imagination.

"That's very nice of you. He likes coming out to Cruise Night. Loves people, but he's not too fond of other dogs. He goads them until they want to fight him, but he's never going to win."

"Yep. Small pup, thinks he's a big dog. In his mind."

Well, in my mind this was a simple recipe for large vet bills. I always kept an eye out for other dogs, ready to pick Rocco up at any moment.

"How much for a CD, Bernie?"

"Oh, they're homemade. Just $10."

That was on par with what other local musicians charged. "Great. I'll take one." I was struggling to get my wallet out of my shoulder bag. The dog was losing his mind, dancing on his hind legs, and pulling on the blue leash. "Settle down, Rocco. We'll walk some more in a minute or two." I knew I sounded exasperated, but sometimes having an 11-year-old perpetual motion machine was tiring.

Bernie and I managed to exchange money and music. I stuck the CD and my wallet into my bag, and said to Roc, "Happy now? Let's go."

But now he wouldn't walk. Usually, he took off like a shot, choking and gagging at the end of the leash when he wanted to head out. He seemed to have a total fascination with Bernie and his 50s restoration. He was sniffing the rear tires, and I held him back in case he had any ideas. But he still kept straining towards the vehicle. Now he was starting a routine of spins and barks.

I shook my head. He usually saved this performance for me, zipping around the apartment, displaying a full repertoire of snarls, growls, and sharp barks, all the while nipping at my ankles. Then dancing away before I could catch him. He'd never yet foamed at the mouth, but I often called him a 'were-poodle' right to his face.

By now he was drawing a crowd. At least everyone was laughing. "What do you feed him, Zora?" someone yelled.

"Is he on something?" asked another bystander.

I admit Rocco looked like I fed him two cats a day with a chaser of amphetamines, but I muttered, "Dry kibble." Next, he dived under the back of the vehicle and began pawing at the undercarriage of the car. I hauled him out, forcing a little laugh, "Oh, Bernie's probably got his shopping in the trunk. Right?" I looked over at Bernie expectantly.

"Nope, no shopping. I like to keep the trunk fresh and clean."

I was getting a funny feeling in the pit of my stomach. I wanted to ask Bernie to open the trunk but not in front of all these people. I grimaced as someone from the crowd took the words right out of my mouth. "Bernie, open it up. What's the little mutt after?"

I was too nervous to object to the terminology. Rocco was 'The Prince' to me.

Bernie shrugged and said, "Sure." We all gathered a bit closer as he fumbled around for the catch and lifted the immense lid of the trunk. Have I mentioned that Rocco is a jumper? Before I could stop him, he leaped straight up, over the license plate reading 'Bertha B', flew into the trunk, and landed on top of Tyler Aston.

23

I have to admit I might have let out a small scream, but it was nothing compared to the middle-aged woman behind me. She was standing with her eyes closed and her mouth open wide, shrieking so loud it was bringing an even larger crowd. Her husband was trying to lead her away, but she was rooted to the asphalt.

In fact, Bernie was almost as bad. He had pushed his shades up onto the top of his head and was yelling, "Bertha, Bertha. Oh, no!" and flapping his arms around helplessly.

As for me, I made a quick move to extricate the dog from the crime scene. Of course, I assumed the worst. I tried not to cringe as I reached over Tyler's inert form to grab Rocco.

The trunk was cavernous. It was easily five to five-and-half feet wide, and a good five feet long, front to back. About two feet of height easily accommodated the young man's body. Someone had placed him on his side facing the front of the car and, other than for the bloody gash on the back of his head, he looked like he was sleeping. Rocco was hopping around like he had springs on his feet and I lost my balance when I reached again for his collar. Horrors! I ended up leaning one hand on Tyler's shoulder. Which was warm.

Suddenly I straightened up and yelled, "Back up! He's not dead!"

I grabbed my phone and dialed 911. "Ambulance and police," I shouted, trying to remain calm. "The back of the Canadian Tire parking lot. Someone's been attacked. Head injury."

I turned around and said sharply to the man with the screaming wife, "Either you move her, or I will." A couple of other women gathered around her and pushed and pulled her further away. I saw that hubby was drinking a blue slushie and thought he could have dumped it on her to bring her to her senses. But that's just me, I guess.

Next, I said to Bernie, "Keep quiet. It's nothing a bit of rug shampoo won't fix. Help me move all these people back a few feet."

He nodded contritely and did as I asked. I could hear the ambulance in the distance, so I did not try to move or revive Tyler.

I quickly took a few photos on my phone, including one that didn't show much of Tyler, just the edge of his clothing. The Whistle was a family publication after all. Next, I turned on a voice recorder app and asked, "When's the last time you looked in the trunk, Bernie?"

"No idea," he looked like he was in shock.

"Where do you park it?"

"In the garage. Where else?"

"Is the garage locked?"

"Yes, of course." But then he paused. He added slowly, "But when I came outside today to open up the garage and get Bertha ready for Cruise Night, something was off." He paused and closed his eyes. Then he looked back at me and said, "I think someone else had been in my garage."

"What makes you say that?"

"I have the overhead lights on a three-way switch. After I bring Bertha back from a run and park her, I always roll the overhead door down and lock it, walk over to the entrance door and open it, then turn the light off. The switch is always left in the 'down' position by that door. But today when I went in there, it was in the 'up' position."

"Bernie, I hate to ask this, but..."

"No! I had no idea he was in there."

"OK, OK. So, do you have any ideas about who could have been in the garage? Or why they would put Tyler in your trunk?"

"No." He looked down. "Not really."

What was that supposed to mean? "Bernie, if you have any suspicions, the sooner you make them public the safer you'll be."

I was pretty sure Tyler had been both secretive and over-confident. At the least. And now look at him. I sure hoped he hadn't tried to leverage his suspicions. I didn't want to think of him as a prospective blackmailer, but he'd certainly pushed someone's buttons.

"It's not that," Bernie said. "I hate to say it but a lot of people have keys. It's a double garage and I often store musical equip-ment like amps and monitors in there. Just temporarily. It makes it easy for the guys to pull up and use their own trucks or vans if we have to move stuff to a gig."

I felt like I was getting precisely nowhere with these ques-tions. All the Bandits had been onstage when Fred was shot. Playing a Johnny Cash cover. It made absolutely no difference how many of them had keys.

I heard loud voices behind me speaking with authority, "Move back, let us through." I shut the recorder off and beck-oned the paramedics over. I explained, "My dog jumped in, and when I went to catch him, I touched the victim by accident.

That's when I realized he was warm and still alive. I'm the one who called you."

"Thank you. Do you know who it is?"

"Yes. His name is Tyler Aston. He's Dr. Aston's son."

"OK, thanks. We'll take it from here."

For such a short woman, Constable Renée Winters had an opera-caliber voice. I heard her and Arni doing their best to move the crowd of curiosity seekers away from the ambulance and the back of Bertha.

I went and stood back beside a car that looked so old that it might have been a Model T. Marley rushed up to me and said, "I leave you alone for five minutes and this is what happens. What's going on? Who are they putting in the ambulance?"

I narrowed my eyes. "I've just about had my fill of this person. Whoever killed the mayor has just about done the same to Tyler. I have no idea how much of this trouble he caused himself."

"I thought you had him pegged for the killer."

"Well, I did for a while. But I had a chat with him yesterday, and I changed my mind. I think he knew who the killer was and either wanted revenge or had decided to use the information."

"Blackmail?"

"Oh, I don't know. I told him to go to the police and to be careful, but I don't think he did either thing."

It wasn't much longer before I saw Arni headed our way. He looked down at Rocco, "I didn't know he was part bloodhound."

"I always thought he would make a fine search and rescue dog. But I meant at earthquake sites in third-world countries, not in the Canadian Tire parking lot."

"All joking aside, if Tyler makes it, he should buy Rocco a nice big steak or something."

I heaved a huge sigh. Marley was looking at me in puzzlement. I said, "I'll tell you later. I need an ice cream cone."

Arni said he would stop by the office first thing in the morning. "Unless you have anything to say now?"

I shook my head and said, "I'm just so glad we found him. I hope Tyler wakes up and can identify who hit him. That would tie everything up, I think."

"I agree. I'm going to follow the ambulance. See you in the morning."

24

D espite a late night and lots of excitement, I couldn't sleep in. I was also very concerned about Tyler, but at least with his parents in the medical field, and Jordan living in town, there would be people who cared for him at his side or nearby.

I knew Arni would be stopping by sometime before 9:00, so 6:00 a.m. seemed like a good time to take my little rescue hero for a stroll. I was so happy that Rocco had persisted with his antics until Bernie opened the trunk. Tyler's assault could very well have had a different ending.

The dog and I wandered around block after block in the cool dawn. We circled through the downtown, took a look along the municipal docks and woke up some ducks, and walked slowly around random blocks of solid old houses shaded by maples and surrounded by spring flowers. After an hour or so, we headed home. Me for a shower, Rocco for a shift of guarding.

I was too restless to be productive in the office, so I permitted myself the ultimate workday treat, sitting at a table in Coyote Coffee. I ordered a latte and a breakfast bagel, the words 'for here' already bringing me a sense of relaxation. I was able to get a seat near the back. I didn't even want to people-watch today.

The owner of the café was a local guy named Curtis King. He was an all-star barista in his own right, and he had made a success of the place. He'd been my tenant for years, and I hoped that would never change. Curtis still looked youthful, with trimmed dark hair and beard and dark-framed glasses. He was tall and thin, and looked like he should be sitting out front with a laptop working on a novel, instead of behind the scenes running a successful small business.

The café had started out with a rugged western vibe, rough board floors, and exposed brick walls. The structural supports were made of tree trunks with the bark still on. Over the years, Curtis had made many nice additions. There was a seating area with couches and armchairs near a rustic-looking gas stove, and also a corner cabinet made from half an old canoe, standing on one end and filled with used books, free for borrowing. The café had numerous nice small wooden tables and chairs, many with charging stations nearby.

Best of all, the coffee was roasted locally, and all the breads and pastries were fresh daily. I read the news on my phone, sipped my coffee, and enjoyed my breakfast. I spotted Arni walking in and ordering a large dark roast in his insulated mug, and gave him a wave. He came over and sat down while I finished up the last of my food and beverage.

"Sorry to make you move, Zora, but we probably need some privacy."

I nodded and gathered up my dishes to put on the counter, and we headed next door to the meeting room.

"First of all, Arni, how is Tyler doing?"

"He woke up briefly and recognized his parents and Jordan. He's sort of drifting in and out, at the moment. The doctors say that all his vital signs are strong, and they expect him to be more wakeful over the next few days. But, at the moment, there's no way we can question him."

"That's not good. I want this person stopped. And I was so hopeful that Tyler would provide the missing piece to the puzzle. Even if we knew where he was attacked, it would help."

"Agreed. We've interviewed Bernie at great length. Eventually, we had to let him go home. The problem is the timetable and, as you said, the location of the assault. I believe that Bernie himself did not hit Tyler and pop him into Big Bertha. Or whatever he calls that car. But I can't figure out how or when the attacker managed to drive up to Bernie's place, in full sight of the house, open the garage, move an unconscious man into the trunk and leave. All without being noticed."

"Is it possible that Tyler was in the trunk since the night before? The killer could have acted after dark more easily."

"Highly unlikely. There was enough air in there to last him a few hours, but we don't think he would have made it around the clock. Bernie tells us he's semi-retired and was home all day yesterday."

"What does he do?"

"He and Jasper are both in the car business."

"I know about Jasper and his used-car empire, but I had never met Bernie until last night. Does he work for his brother?"

"Nope. He has a thriving auto body repair shop on the way out the north end of town."

I smiled, "Well, that makes total sense. No wonder that Chrysler 300 is such a beauty. He must enjoy having a few more hours a week for his hobby. Even semi-retirement is nice." But learning about Bernie's business, however successful it might be, was not bringing us closer to the killer.

"Did you have any luck tracking down key-holders to his garage? He told me he had spread them around quite a bit, over the years."

"We're on it. But it's going to be a long shot. The Billytown Bandits have been around forever, and often changed personnel."

Suddenly, I had a thought. It may just have been the nourishing breakfast, but I was pretty sure I could help with one aspect of this mystery. Timing. I picked up my phone. "Can you give me Bernie's number? I want to try something."

"I don't see why not." Arni dictated the digits to me and I keyed them in.

"Good morning, Bernie," I said when he answered. "This is Zora Flynn, from Cruise Night. How are you feeling today?"

Bernie had to take a while to explain his distress about Bertha, and I made sympathetic noises. I then said, "I have to compliment you. I had a chance to play that CD of yours. It's a lot of fun, and really well done. I especially liked the live tracks."

Arni was making 'hurry-up' motions, so I waited for a few seconds and then interrupted Bernie's reminiscences about the various saloons of Muskoka where he and the Bandits had played. It was actually quite an entertaining local history lesson, and I made a note to ask the reporters to do a story. Once we finished with our crime-fighting. "Bernie, you have some really fine banjo skills. You must love playing."

Before he could get too carried away with a lifetime of country music anecdotes, I said, "I gather you're semi-retired. That must give you more time to practice. Uh huh. Can I ask if you were playing the banjo yesterday afternoon? You were? Yes, I'm sure time just flies by when you love music that much. Good job your neighbors aren't too close, right?" I teased him.

That set Bernie off on a soliloquy about the pros and cons of the various amps he'd owned over the years. I gently cut him off. "Bernie, I have to get back to work. Can you please let me know the next time you're playing anywhere? I'd love to attend. OK, thanks."

I looked triumphantly over at Arni. "He was practicing in the basement for at least two hours yesterday afternoon. From about 2:00 to 4:00 and maybe longer. With the banjo plugged into an amp. I don't think there's any way he would've heard a vehicle pull up to his garage."

Arni rubbed his hands over his eyes. "Wow, I need some sleep. But this is fantastic, Zora. A huge help. Now that we know we're looking at that narrower timeframe, we have a chance of tracking Tyler's movements. We can question suspects and we can even canvas residents on Bernie's road."

The more I thought about it, the more chilling this new information seemed. "It also certainly tells us about the person behind this nightmare."

Arni nodded and said, "For sure. Someone is very familiar with the place. Imagine. You've just knocked a guy out and want somewhere to put him. How many people would think about driving to Bernie's, breaking into the garage, popping the trunk, and dumping Tyler inside?"

"Nerves of steel, as they say. Everything was done in broad daylight. This killer is cold. Not to mention they've now possibly framed Bernie for the attack on Tyler, and maybe for the murder as well."

I continued, "Arni, what about the method of the attacks? One was a gun, and one was a blow to the back of the head. Could there be two people involved? Or maybe I've just been reading too many mystery novels."

"It's something to think about. But I believe it was the same person. It could be just as simple as the fact that he wanted to get rid of the gun immediately, and doesn't own another one."

"Well, thank goodness for that," I exclaimed.

Arni slapped his hands down on the table and stood up. "OK, I have to get going. Thanks again."

"Just catch this guy," I replied.

25

I was expecting the reporters to arrive any minute, so I didn't move from my spot in the meeting room. My brain was buzzing with the mystery of the mayor's death followed by the attack on Tyler, but we still had a paper to produce. The first order of business had better be to formalize a story list.

"Good morning," they both said in a chorus and slid into seats across from me. From the expectant looks on their faces, I figured they were aware that I had news. I didn't keep them in suspense. Once again, I sent Brady my photos. I asked him to post the least graphic of the shots of Tyler in the trunk of Bertha on the website.

We took about half an hour to come up with a list of the main stories that would be included in next Wednesday's paper.

I said I'd do an article on the discovery of Tyler, and I asked Brady to go and get a comment from his parents. "I'll trade you," I said, "I interviewed Carlton Miner and I'll send a draft over to you for your big story on the bylaw scandal. If that's what we can call it."

"Might as well," he laughed. "I'm not sure I have proof of

anything, but people are losing patience with the existing process, that's for sure."

"Well, I think there is something going on. If you could have seen Carlton's face when I asked him if someone was giving him orders... But that's for later. One step at a time."

Olivia spoke up. "I had a chance to speak to Sonny Rigg. Two things. He doesn't have any insight into who killed Fred. He said that because the band was playing at the time of his death, he never left the sound board, and was totally focused on tech stuff. But."

She smiled and pushed her hairband back, "There's more."

I bit my tongue and Brady said, "Come on, what?"

"Sonny seems to be going through a stage right now. He can't stand living at home and says his mother is driving him crazy. He's only 16, still in school, no job, and obviously can't afford to move out. But he was very talkative when it came to his mother's political ambitions. He says she's obsessed with the council, and it's gotten worse. She plans to run for mayor to replace Fred."

"Nice, Olivia," I congratulated her. "Have you had time to talk to Leona about this?"

"Oh, yes. And I got a big fat 'no comment.' But I'm going to do the story anyway. As far as I can see, it's still news."

"I agree. Did you record your conversation with Sonny?"

"Yes, for sure."

"Then you can refer to him as a 'reliable source' instead of using his name. But we should be getting in touch with the other councilors to see if they have plans as well. This could be interesting. We can divide up the list. Let me just see where Whitmore lives. I know the general area."

I pulled my laptop over in front of me, opened up Maps, and typed in Cowboy Whitmore's address off the main town website.

Sure enough, the big, blue dot locating Whitmore's hobby farm appeared on the screen, on the northern edge of town. I expanded the view to get a better look at the route through the rural area and to my surprise a red pin popped up identifying a business. Practically next door.

Driving northward from downtown Williamsport and making a left, you'd go a mile or two before first reaching the business and then Whitmore's place. I was puzzled. I didn't know of any shops out that way. I clicked on the red pin and murmured, "Well, well, well." In a text box on the screen were the words, 'Bernie's Restorations.'

I thought it might be well worth my while to pay a visit to Cowboy's ranch. I said, "One of you can take McShane and I'll speak to Whitmore. Also, we have Sylvia Blaine to contact. I'll leave her to you."

Sylvia was the fourth town councilor. She'd been off our radar for a while, because she hadn't attended the political meeting where Fred had died and, although I'd seen her at the funeral, she hadn't attended the reception. Probably a wise decision on her part.

I couldn't imagine Sylvia being entangled in Fred's murder, and certainly not behind the attack on Tyler. I also didn't see her as a participant in our incipient bylaw scandal. She was a petite woman about my age and was a retired school teacher. If there was an environmental issue, she was tireless. And fierce. But otherwise, she tended to be level-headed and a calming influence on council.

Olivia said, "We can do that. Zora, I know you asked us not to contact certain people but is it OK if I follow up with Jasper Butler? I just want to find out when the riding association will meet to finish their voting."

"That sounds fine," I said absently. "I think we're all good to go."

We all retreated to our respective offices, but I didn't stay there long. I went upstairs and got Rocco, and then went out the back door to my car. Our last couple of outings had been full of drama. I couldn't guarantee that this trip would be any different, but I vowed to lock the dog up securely before leaving the car this time. Just to be on the safe side, I put Roc in his crate on the back seat before setting out. He didn't mind it, as long as the road was smooth. If not, he was vocal in his objections.

I headed north on Main Street and then carried on out of town. After about 15 minutes, I made the left turn onto Maple Hill Road. It was another beautiful day, with the sun dappling the road in moving patterns of light and shadow. Maple Hill was living up to its name, and the gravel road was filled with climbs, valleys, twists, and turns.

Various moans and whines could be heard from the back seat. Rocco loved a long drive on a straight four-lane highway. He was not a fan of the backroads. The Prince continued to sing the blues as I carried on towards Councilor Whitmore's place. Every so often, I leaned back and directed a stern 'Shh!' into the rear of the car.

Although it felt a bit remote, being this far from town, the area was quite built up. Not like a subdivision, but there was a pretty house or hunt camp every minute or so. Like the area where Ollie Hanson lived, Maple Hill Road was a mix of small cottages and large new homes. Everyone had a nice spacious lot, and the forest surrounding each residence had created a lot of privacy.

There was no other traffic, so I slowed right down, keeping an eye out my left window and trying to spot Bernie's place. Soon enough I saw the word Butler on a shiny red mailbox and slowed even more. Bernie had a nice old ranch-style bungalow with white siding and green trim with matching green shutters. Across the yard were two structures, a two-car garage and a large barn-sized workshop. The garage wasn't super close to the house and I could easily see how someone could back up to the building and move Tyler without being noticed.

I cruised on by and, as I suspected from the map I had seen online, the Whitmore place was the next property on my left. The councilor had a large chalet-style house and a variety of outbuildings in the same style. Very picturesque. I pulled into the driveway and waited while an insane border collie circled my car. That animal's reputation had preceded him. I made a mental note to watch my step once I got out of the vehicle.

Between the collie's barking and Rocco chiming in, I was relieved to see the councilor striding towards me. I opened the windows and shut the engine off, hopping out before I went deaf.

26

Whitmore was living up to his nickname. He was wearing worn jeans, a denim shirt, and a white cowboy hat. He was a friendly-looking man, a little younger than me, with a tanned face and out-of-style aviator glasses. I took a curious look at his boots. Just regular steel-toed work boots covered in a variety of dubious substances.

"Hi, Zora," he said. "What brings you out this way? It's lucky you caught me. I just got back from the dentist."

I held back from asking him right away if he had killed the mayor and bashed Tyler Aston over the head. I had thought Whitmore would be at work. I was really just interested in checking out the proximity of his house to that of Bernie Butler. But now that he was standing right in front of me, I thought I might as well go ahead with the interview. I'd be holding up my end of the deal with the reporters.

"Hello, Councilor. It was a nice day for a drive, and I thought I'd see if you were around. We're working on a number of stories, and I wonder if I could ask you a couple of questions."

"Sure, no problem. Let's go and sit on the porch."

I was sure hoping there was a screened porch somewhere.

Blackflies were already crawling into the short, buzzed hair around my ears. On the other hand, I didn't really want to stay. "Oh, that's OK. It won't take long."

Then I was inspired. I had on some pretty sturdy boots myself and felt I could handle a bit of a stroll. "But, if you don't think it's an imposition, I've never seen your horses." I thought if Cowboy got into character as the proud owner of a herd of mini-horses, he might be more relaxed and let his guard down when I started asking questions.

His eyes lit up. "Well, you're in for a treat," he said. "Come right this way."

As we walked, I outlined the two stories we were working on. "So, if possible, question number one is your comment on the death of Fred Phipps. Our article, since we're a weekly, is turning into more of a tribute. So if you have a comment, we would be happy to include it."

"Of course," he said. "Fred was a tremendous community booster and a great political leader. He will be missed. I think people forget how much he did over the years for the town of Williamsport. During his three terms in office, many town improvements went ahead, things we might take for granted now. I think his death was a terrible tragedy, and I hope the police are making progress in finding the culprit."

"Cowboy, I probably don't have to remind you that there was quite a scene at the funeral reception. We're asking everyone involved for a comment. Do you have anything to say in response to the women who were complaining about your dog? Do you think there is a problem with bylaw enforcement in Williamsport?"

"You know, Zora, I wish those women had brought their concerns to me first, before calling the town. If my dog has been wandering around off the property, I take responsibility for that. Ever since that morning at the funeral, I've been keeping a closer eye on him. I like to let him run free, but now I'm making sure that he's in his pen when I'm not outside."

Hmm. This sure sounded like a guy with higher political aspirations. Talk about making all the right noises.

"Last question. We've been making inquiries about the future membership of the town Council. Sadly, there's a vacancy to fill. Have you given this any thought?"

"I hadn't planned to make a public announcement quite this soon. If you're going to quote me, could you please make that clear? But, yes, I would like to let my name stand as a candidate to replace Fred as mayor."

"Thanks very much," I said. I made a bit of a show about putting my phone back in my bag, but I did not turn the voice recorder app off. "I guess you had a bit of excitement in the neighborhood yesterday."

"Unbelievable! The police were here half the night. I simply can't imagine that Bernie Butler would be involved in this type of crime. We've been friends and neighbors for years."

"Fortunately for Bernie, I think the police are looking else-where for answers. Did you even know Tyler Aston?"

"Oh, sure. By the time the kids get through high school, I usually know most of them, at least to see them."

"I don't know him at all. What kind of a guy is he?"

"Pretty average. I never would have pegged him for law school, but I wish him all the best if that's what he wants."

By this time, we had walked up the driveway, past the garage, and through the backyard. On the way, I couldn't help noticing that Cowboy had a nice, big pickup truck with a cap, parked beside his horse trailer. How easy would it have been to put Tyler into the back of the truck, put the tailgate up and drive next door?

I couldn't help myself. I had to laugh in delight. As we turned the corner, a panoramic series of neatly fenced farm fields opened up. In the foreground was a small barn and walking around were a dozen of the cutest horses I had ever encountered. They were all about three feet tall but that was the only commonality. There were brown horses and black horses. Some were gray, some had spots. They had manes and tails of varying lengths. Some were contentedly standing around a hay rack munching on the contents. Others were out in the field grazing, and a couple were chasing each other like big puppies.

The sight of them also interrupted my train of thought. Could the owner of these sweet little animals also be a killer? That was a very thought-provoking question.

"Beautiful spot. And the horses are the best. Talk about cuteness overload."

"Yes, we love them. I know it's a business, but to be honest, I'd probably keep them anyway."

"The farm. Is it one of the original ones?"

"Yes, it is. The acreage has been sub-divided a bit, but the farm dates from the mid-1800s."

"Every time I see one of these historic homesteads, I can't help but marvel at the work that the original settlers must have done to clear the area, build their home and run things with no machinery."

"Me, too. It's enough work just to keep the poplar and pine saplings out of the fields, mend the fences, and look after the horses. And I'm not even really farming."

We went over to the paddock fence and I got to feed the ponies some kind of horse treat that Cowboy gave me. I sure hoped he wasn't guilty. I might want to come back here someday.

"Well, I better be going," I said. "I have my dog out for a ride in the car, and I'm sure he's sick of snapping at the flies by now."

We turned around and headed back, and I thanked Cowboy for the tour. What a great way to spend a June afternoon.

Once I was in the car and driving back out Maple Hill Road, I couldn't help but think of the two Whitmores I had now met. Cowboy 1 was a smooth-talking politician with aspirations to higher office, even if that was to be mayor of a small town. Cowboy 2 owned a bunch of adorable small horses. And a bunch of shovels and other tools that could be used to knock someone out. And a pickup truck suitable for transporting an unconscious man.

I thought about it a little longer and decided that it almost didn't matter. Both Cowboys had a motive as far as I could see.

27

A s Friday wore on, I couldn't help anticipating a call or text from Darius Bell. I had missed seeing him last weekend and was hoping he would be headed back up to cottage country soon. Sure enough, as I was driving back to the office, I heard my phone chime. As soon as I got parked, I gave it a look and with a smile texted back, "Yay, see you for dinner."

I was happy and excited at the thought of heading out at the end of the workday. Even though it took less than an hour to drive to Darius's cottage, it felt like traveling to another world. And Darius himself was very special to me. How many women my age get to fall in love all over again? Yes, I valued my independence and was proud of my success in business, but our relationship added spice and sparkle to my day-to-day life.

Rocco skipped along from the parked car, through my new back gate and into the building. I headed straight upstairs, to pack an overnight bag with some of my new clothes, and some wine. Darius knew my beverage of choice, after white wine, was iced tea and he always had some in the fridge. But I liked to bring him a bottle of his favorite red anyway. I also kept my eye out at the Farmers' Market for treats to bring along. Maybe some local maple syrup, homemade jam, or even smoked meats and cheeses for an appetizer or lunch. We had two craft breweries in town and shopping for someone else was a great excuse to visit there and pick up some beer, especially in the summer months.

We were back in the car and on the road with no further delays, this time heading south. Muskoka boasted over 1000 lakes, but few Ontario locations compared to the Big Four: Lake Muskoka, Lake Joseph, Compass Lake, and Lake Rosseau. They shared a storied past that included the rustic roots of today's tourism, but stayed in the spotlight in the present day with huge spreads owned by movie stars, NHL players, and at least one tech magnate.

Darius had gotten really lucky. He told his real estate agent that he wasn't too fussy when it came to budget. But he didn't want anything over 2000 square feet. Now, there was an interesting filter for a property search in this area. He'd used his funds to buy privacy as opposed to a northern mansion.

The getaway had about 500 yards of Big Lake frontage, down a long twisty driveway that had Rocco whining and complaining from the back seat on every visit. The cottage itself would have seemed huge when it was built nearly a century ago, but was small potatoes when compared to what wealthy people tended to construct these days.

I bumped along down the drive and parked. Darius walked out to greet me and I was waiting to see his expression when he saw my haircut. I was delighted and relieved when he threw his head back and laughed, while saying, "I love it. It's totally you!"

"Thanks. I was a little worried that you wouldn't recognize me," I joked, and then added, "You're looking pretty good yourself, handsome."

That was true, for sure. Darius had changed into some black basketball shorts that showed off his tanned muscular legs, and his steel-gray hair was swept back off his angular face. He had on an older Raptors t-shirt and sports sandals. He was obviously ready for a relaxing weekend.

I had to admit I was equally fond of the Darius that wore sleek navy blue suits or city-casual clothing. But if I was honest with myself, what I really looked forward to was our time together. Regardless of wardrobe. I felt I had somehow managed to meet a man with whom I could be myself. What a great feeling that was.

Together we headed up to the main entrance. Rocco sped off in search of the squirrels that were welcoming, um, scolding him. A deep porch overlooked a long grassy lawn and then the lake. It extended across the full width of the building, and had huge stonework pillars, with a central front door.

The cottage had dark brown siding, white trim, gable windows on the second floor and, best of all, a huge screened room at one end of the building. There was a reason that these spaces had come to be known as 'Muskoka rooms,' and that had to do with the bountiful insect population, especially in June.

We made our way through the house and then back out into the screened porch where Darius had the barbecue running and a table full of dinner food. In the time he'd owned the cottage he had made some very useful connections nearby. He had efficiently organized everything from housekeeping to catering to maintenance.

He handed me a glass of wine with a 'Cheers,' and a kiss. "It's so great to be back."

"I missed you, too," I replied.

As we sat and looked out over the lake, silvery and calm as glass in the early evening, he said, "I've been so curious. You said something had happened that I wouldn't believe."

"And more." By the time I had told him about Fred's death, the funeral, the fire, and the attack on Tyler, we were well on the way through dinner. I tried to keep the tone of my account light, even though these were very serious matters.

Trust Darius to come right to the point, "Any impact on advertising?"

"It's too early to tell. But I've told the reporters about my concerns. It's only fair. Seriously, the sooner the real killer is identified, and I can get out of the spotlight, the happier I'll be." I handed Rocco a scrap of chicken and he smiled back. "In the meantime, we've been keeping track of our ideas. It's doubling as a list of possible stories for the paper, and possible suspects."

"Lists? Really? Come with me. I don't think I've shown you the changes to my office."

We went upstairs and there might have been joking about etchings. But the office was amazing. The old cottage had started out with five bedrooms, and it appeared that there were now three, plus an office. The dividing wall between two rooms had been removed, creating one big airy space with a view of the treetops in the back yard.

I was expecting Darius to reveal a cutting-edge technology set-up that would miraculously collate and analyze my list of suspects. Was I ever wrong. The big reveal was an entire wall painted with whiteboard paint, and a basket with about 50 dry-erase markers. It was like my office board on steroids.

"Fantastic. I can show you everything on here." I took a blue marker, walked to the left side of the wall, and wrote: Jordan Phipps, Tyler Aston. Then I took a red marker and added Ollie Hanson, mainly so I could tell Darius the bear story. I had a look at the other colors and chose green for Leona Rigg, Sonny Rigg, Cowboy Whitmore, and Jed McShane. Below in orange I thought I might as well scrawl Sylvia Blaine. Finally, I made a note of Moose Logan and Carlton Miner. What the heck. I also wrote down Bernie Butler's name.

Then in the center of a curly purple cloud drawing, I added my own name and a smiley face.

Darius looked my list over and said, "So, I'm missing the context for all these people. Is it OK if I make another chart with some columns?"

"Fine. We need one space for their relationship to Fred, and one for motive. We already worked out, that at the time of the killing, everyone on the list had the opportunity. So, we started looking at motive instead. Also, beside Carlton's name, we added a bunch of citizens who are mad at him and ranting about municipal corruption."

"OK, let's do it." I let him go to town with his markers.

When he was done, I added a fourth column with a big '?' for the title. He looked over at me and I said, "This is where I tell you why I think some of these people are not serious contenders. I told him about Ollie's hatred of firearms, Moose's impetuous temperament, and Tyler's insinuations that he knew the guilty party. I also felt it was safe to remove Jordan, Sonny, and Sylvia. And poor Bernie. He would never have defiled Bertha!

We spent quite a while filling out the third column, and adding in the possible motivation linking the more viable suspects to the late mayor.

"What do you think?" I asked. We had been busy for nearly an hour and I knew that there was a luscious-looking strawberry cheesecake in the fridge for dessert.

"Well, I'm no police officer, let alone a profiler. Some of these people seem like definite possibilities." Then he hesitated.

"And?"

"I think there's someone missing. Someone with an intense and personal reason for killing Fred Phipps. Why did Fred himself have to die? What was he doing or going to do? What was he going to say? How could he have seriously hurt someone?"

I had a sinking feeling. Had I discounted Olivia too soon? Had her youth, petite stature, and honest demeanor blinded me to the possibility that she and Fred were involved in an obsessive and explosive relationship? And not the more or less innocent flirtation she had described? I wasn't sure enough to break a confidence, and I left her off the list.

Instead, I commented, "Funny, that's why we had Jordan on the list. And why we took her off as well. Family dynamics can be very dangerous. But at the same time, we just couldn't imagine her killing her father, and in that way. If only he hadn't been such a nice guy, this would all be easier."

We looked at the big wall of suspects for a little longer and then headed off for more enjoyable pursuits.

Saturday dawned cool and overcast and although we were tempted to stay in bed all day, we didn't. Our weekends together at the cottage were spent quietly together.

When I visited Darius in the city, we were more social, going out for meals, attending events, and so forth. But when we were at the lake, we tended to keep to ourselves and enjoy the natural setting. Even for me, it was a treat. Although I lived north of the 45th parallel, I was a town resident. Being at the lake was completely different.

We decided to pack up a picnic, using some of the leftovers from the night before, and go for a long canoe paddle. Rocco sat quietly in the center of the watercraft, or sometimes up front in the bow with me, his black nose sniffing the air. The lake was quiet since the big crowds wouldn't arrive until after the July long weekend. And the breeze was perfect, enough to keep the bugs away but not enough to make me work too hard. We made our way slowly around the rocky shore and, even on a cloudy day like this one, each new view was postcard-pretty.

When we got back, Darius made a roaring fire in the living room to take the chill off, and we lounged around before having a quiet dinner. The fresh air and exercise made me drowsy and it was hard to recall when I had last felt so relaxed. I looked up at him and said, "You know, I hope you're as happy as I am."

He smiled and placed a kiss on the top of my head. "More than you could ever know. This is what keeps me going. I love my work, but I feel like a new person since buying this place. It's what you first said. Balance. I always think there's no way I can go out of town and switch off. And then I do."

"And the world doesn't end, correct?"

"You got it."

Ironically, it was me who ended up having to break the spell.

unday morning started out as usual, with a lazy coffee and breakfast on the screen porch. Darius said he would wait until early afternoon before heading for the highway. We were just talking about maybe doing some gardening when to my surprise my cellphone rang. The signal in this location was not reliable and I rarely got any calls.

"Hello?" I said.

"Hello, Zora?"

"Yes, speaking."

"I'm so sorry to bother you but..." Darius looked over at me with a question. I shrugged. I didn't know who it was.

"Can I ask who's calling?" It was a man and he sounded a bit upset.

"Sorry, sorry. It's Richard Park. Olivia's father."

"Oh, hi Richard. Is everything OK?"

"I'm not sure. I think Olivia's missing. No one else agrees. But I just know something is the matter."

I sat up straight in my chair. I didn't want to think the worst, but after the last week or so, I couldn't help it.

"I'm calling you to see if you might know where she is."

"When did you last see her?"

"Yesterday at breakfast. Can you tell me what assignments she's working on? Is she involved in anything dangerous that I don't know about?"

"No, absolutely not. We even talked about that. I'm doing the interviews of anyone connected with the recent incidents myself."

"OK. This is going to sound pushy and over-protective, but I don't care. Do you know if she was seeing anyone? Maybe she has a boyfriend she didn't want to tell us about. Maybe she's with him."

"No. I don't think so. We were talking about that the other day at work and joking about the lack of suitable men in town. I think she and Brady were a bit shocked that I would even say so."

I shot Darius a grin and patted his thigh.

"Richard, I think you should contact the police."

"I did. They said she's an adult and can come and go as she pleases. I'm not arguing with that. I tried to tell them we don't monitor her every move. She just lives at home. What if she had an apartment with roommates? It would be the same thing."

"Can I ask when you were expecting her?"

"Olivia is very considerate. If she's not going to be home for dinner, she always contacts her mother. They message each other during the day anyway. More just humorous stuff, or pictures of food. Whatever. Not the details of her personal life. Anyway, we were a bit worried when she didn't arrive for dinner or get in touch. Then we were out with friends for the evening. A birthday party. We tried several times to reach her, but there was never an answer."

"I'm so sorry to hear all this. It must have been a long night."

"Yes."

I was getting choked up because Richard's voice was breaking. I took a deep breath and said, "I'm at a friend's place myself. I'm going to leave in a few minutes. When I get a better signal, I'll call Brady and ask him to meet me at the office. You're welcome to meet us there around noon if you want to."

I didn't say so, but I would definitely be getting in touch with Arni myself. This whole situation didn't sound good at all.

"I will. Thank you very much."

I picked up my coffee mug for one last sip and said, "Well, I guess you heard most of that?"

"Yes. And I agree with you. Something's wrong. Is there anything I can do?"

"I don't think so. But I'm going to get ready and head back to town. Sorry to take off early." We shared a few more minutes together and then I headed for the shower.

I was very familiar with the route back home, and knew that the massive rock cuts and wilderness lakes would make getting a signal difficult. I waited about half an hour and voice-dialed Brady. I explained about Richard Park's call and he said, "I agree. In my opinion Olivia is just a regular person. She's happy with her life, gets along with everyone, likes her work. I can't even begin to think of a reason why she wouldn't go home for dinner or not answer her phone. I'm sure something's happened. This is terrible. You're in the car?"

"Yes, I'm only 15 or 20 minutes from the office."

"Good, see you there."

My next call was to Arni. I was so glad he picked up. After all, in his books I guess I was still a suspect in Fred's murder.

"Good morning," I said. We exchanged a few pleasantries and then I asked, "Have you been to the station today? I know it's Sunday."

"No. I was at church and now I'm barbecuing. Trying to barbecue," he said pointedly.

"I know it's your day off, but I took a chance that you might like to know." And ideally do something, I added privately. "My reporter, Olivia Park, is missing. I'm meeting her father and Brady at the office shortly. Just passing along the information. You're welcome to join us."

I listened to him and then answered, "Yes, Richard went to the station, but they sent him away." Good job I had the phone on speaker and not against my ear, because Arni raised his voice. "I agree. See you shortly."

Soon we were all seated around the meeting room table. Except for Rocco who lounged in his office bed in the sun.

Arni opened his notebook, and asked Richard to repeat everything he had already told me. Then he looked over at me. "Was Olivia working this weekend?"

"Yes. It was her turn."

"OK, so where was she going?"

I had already compared notes with Brady, and we had come up with a short list. "First, she was going to take a picture at the mall where the Soccer League players were doing a car wash and the fire department was sending the pumper truck to help out. Next was the Strawberry Social at the church on Main Street. Finally, the Craft Beer Festival at Riverside Park."

Arni gestured at the whiteboard story list. OK, suspect list. "Was Olivia talking to any of these people?"

"No. I'm continuing to interview anyone connected with the death of Fred Phipps myself. The last person she interviewed was Sonny Rigg, sometime last week. It was straightforward, and he mainly discussed the fact that he's annoyed with his mother."

I looked up at the list and frowned. "You know, there's one name that's not there. Because the person didn't have any connection to Fred Phipps. On Friday at our meeting, Olivia asked if she could go ahead and contact Jasper Butler about when the Conservatives are going to finish up their nomination process."

"So this is the brother of Bernie, the car owner from Cruise Night?"

"That's right. But I don't know that it's relevant. I don't want to waste your time."

"Not a problem. I'll send someone to speak to him right away. At the very least, it might help us establish her movements between Saturday morning and now."

We all nodded, and Arni continued, "Anyone know where Olivia's vehicle is?"

We all looked blankly at each other, then back at Arni, and shook our heads. Richard said, "It's not at home."

Brady hopped up. "I can be over at the park in two minutes. I'll check along the street on my way. But I think she would have left the car down by the river and walked back to the church."

He texted me in less than five minutes. Olivia's car was in the lot at Riverside Park. I don't know why I felt good about his success in finding it. A split second later my stomach turned over. This was the worst possible news. Richard buried his head in his hands and Arni stood up. He said, "Thanks for getting the ball rolling. Gotta go."

29

I could only imagine the stress and heartbreak going on at the home of Richard and Liz Park. I had a rough night myself. I wasn't even in the mood for an early morning walk through town. Rare for me. I took Rocco around the block, locked him upstairs to guard, and was on the doorstep of Coyote Coffee when Curtis came to open.

I got my usual latte, and then went next door to open up the office. I was too restless to settle down, so I sat at Barbara's desk and watched the street come to life. Who in the world could have taken Olivia? This was a friendly town with very little major crime. Now we'd seen a murder, an arson, and a serious assault in just a week. I was driving myself crazy worrying about what had happened to Olivia. 'Taken.' It was such a euphemism. I was so afraid for her.

Had Olivia somehow figured out who was responsible for Fred's death? I just couldn't see her tackling a murder suspect on her own. She knew we had a good relationship with Arni, and she also knew Brady and I would support her. At least I hoped she did. I was so frustrated. I couldn't think of anything to do that would make a difference. I was no closer to a solution to the original crimes, and I certainly had no idea how to find Olivia. And time was ticking by.

As I sat there getting more upset by the minute, I saw Marley approaching. I got up and opened the door. Marley stepped aside and to my surprise ushered in a small older woman. "Good morning," I said.

"Hi there, Zora. I'd like to introduce Marion Leger. She's just told me some interesting news. Information I think you might like to hear."

I didn't know if this would be useful or simply a distraction. Either way would be fine, I reflected. I was getting nowhere fast on my own. "Please come in. Let's go back to the meeting room. Mrs. Leger, can I get you anything?"

Marion Leger was a tiny birdlike woman with her hair pinned back into a bun of flyaway white hair. Her eyes were dark and bright, behind small gold-framed glasses. She smiled and shook her head. As we sat down, she looked around curiously, but still didn't say a word. Her hands were restless, and she patted her hair, smoothed the jacket of her beige pantsuit, and straightened her handbag on her lap.

Marley spoke up, "Zora, Marion came to meet with me this morning. I do the books for her church group." She smiled over at the woman and added, "They donate so much money to the community. They're a regular fundraising machine. Such hard workers." Again, Marion smiled and patted her hair.

"Naturally, we got talking about the recent events in town. We were saying how sad it was, about the death of Mayor Phipps, and what a great leader he was. Marion, do you think you could carry on and tell Zora what you told me?"

Marion cleared her throat and adjusted her collar. Her voice came out hardly louder than a whisper. "I've always been interested in politics. My late husband was very active in the Liberal party and I've continued to be involved with the local riding association."

Marley nodded encouragingly, and so did I.

Marion continued, "I'm the secretary. We had an executive meeting the week before last, so of course I was there. Fred was our special guest. He'd agreed to let his name stand as our candidate. We would have had a nomination meeting of course, but we were thrilled that such an honest and well-loved local politician would enter the race. We had no doubt that he would win the nomination. He would have been our candidate in the next election and very likely our next Member of Provincial Parliament. It's such a tragedy."

Although I'd had to strain to hear her voice, there was no mistaking the contents of this bombshell of an announcement. My jaw must have dropped. I closed my mouth and reached for my phone.

"Marion, was this public knowledge?" I asked.

Marion made a twittering sort of noise and patted her hair back in place. "I don't think so. I mean it wasn't a secret, but we all agreed to make a formal announcement at a later date. Today actually. Oh! I don't know if I should've said anything to Marley."

"I'm sure it's fine. Please don't worry," I said, and Marley made sympathetic noises as well.

Marion continued, "We're aware that Mondays and Tuesdays, that is, today and tomorrow, are when you write up the stories for the paper, and the association president was going to stop by with Fred to speak to you in person. And also announce the date for our nomination meeting." Her eyes filled with tears, and she added in a feathery whisper. "But that won't be happening."

I called Arni's cellphone and hoped that he would pick up.

Unfortunately, I got his voice mail. "Arni, it's Zora. Please call me as soon as you can. It's urgent."

I stood up and said, "Marion, I can't thank you enough. This is more helpful than I can say." I was hesitant to go into the details of the present crisis with a stranger, but I couldn't think of a polite way to send Marion on her way and have Marley stay, so I let them both go.

Where was Brady anyway? It was going on towards ten o'clock and in two-plus years I'd never seen him late for a Monday meeting. I followed my guests out to the reception area and waved as they started walking back to the accounting office. At least Barbara was on duty. I waited until the door shut and collapsed in one of the visitors' chairs. Barbara looked up in surprise and said, "Are you OK?"

"Not even close," I replied. "Have you heard from Brady?"

"No. What's wrong?"

She paled as I filled her in about the weekend's events. "What? I can't believe it. Olivia's, like, kidnapped?"

"I have no idea. No one has seen her since Saturday at breakfast and her car was left down at the park. And she's not picking up her phone. Now I have new information for Arni, and he's not answering. And Brady is missing in action, too. I mean, have you ever heard of him being late?"

"Never. What can I do?"

"Keep trying Arni on his cell and at the station. I'm going to keep dialing Brady."

As soon as I sat down in my office, I called Bernie. Since no one else seemed to be available to take my urgent calls.

"Hey Bernie, Zora Flynn again. Fine thanks. I just have a quick question. Was your brother Jasper ever in your band?"

I had to hold the phone away as Bernie hooted in my ear. "Nah. He can't play a thing. And he can't hold a tune. Sounds like a raven if he tries to sing."

Rats! I was so sure I was onto something. I couldn't think why brothers would share their garage keys as a matter of course, but if Jasper had been in the band, he would have had one like the other musicians. But then Bernie's next words gave me a flicker of hope.

"But he sometimes helps us out with moving equipment to gigs. Like a roadie. But don't tell him I said that."

"No. I won't." I said. Now I crossed my fingers and asked, "So at some point, he might have had a key to the garage?"

"Oh, probably. I likely gave him one a while ago."

I was ecstatic but I tried to keep my voice level. "Thank you so much, Bernie. Talk to you soon."

If I was right, he'd be getting interviewed by more people than me, in the very near future.

I picked up my cell phone to try Brady for the twentieth time when Barbara shouted, "Arni. Line 1."

"Thanks, now keep trying Brady. Please."

30

I picked up the phone extension and said, "Any news?"

"No," he replied.

"Did you ever go and see Jasper Butler? It's important."

"Yes. An officer went out there just after noon yesterday. Butler was home, he invited him in. He said he didn't know Olivia and hadn't seen her."

"Well, I think he's lying. I have no idea why, because I can't imagine how Olivia managed to get herself into this much trouble. But ever since my visit with Ollie Hanson, we were leaning towards someone from Fred's political world as the killer. We were just looking at the wrong group. We were looking at the local council instead of provincial politics."

I told him about Marley and Marion's visit, and the astonishing news they had shared with me. "So, imagine you're Jasper. But instead of being a normal small-town politician, you're obsessed with your party's publicity, image, and of course with winning elections. But you hide it well, taking on leadership roles behind the scene, boosting your party whenever you get the chance. Not only that, but you've aligned yourself with a winning team. For decades you haven't had too much stress or struggle. You've never had to fight. But even though you're gratified and proud, you're always on guard, always ready to defend the honor of your party. You might even think that the party's success is entirely due to you. You're the king-maker. Everything will fall to pieces without you. You need to totally control your world."

"That's nuts. Who lives like that?"

"Jasper, I think."

Arni started speculating along the same lines. "So, sometime just before the big conservative meeting with all that hoopla and party fanfare, he somehow gets wind of Fred's intention to run as the Liberal candidate. He might be crazy but he's not stupid. He knows Fred is popular and has a perfect track record in local politics. He would be unbeatable."

"Exactly. I think Jasper became obsessed with getting Fred to switch horses. He would want the mayor to run as a Tory, not a Liberal. And he certainty didn't want to have to face off against him in the next election. Jasper might have started out all friendly and persuasive in his dealings with Fred, but the night of the nomination meeting at the Legion, he crossed a line. When Jasper followed Fred into the men's room, Fred blew up. He had reached the end of his rope and was feeling harassed. That's why he was venting, in what he thought was an empty room, and that's why he spoke to Jasper the way he did. And sadly, once Jasper heard the way Fred spoke to him, he decided the only solution was to kill him."

"This all sounds plausible. So, what you're saying is that because Jasper couldn't persuade Fred to change parties, he killed him so he couldn't give the opposition an edge."

"Yes. That's what I think is behind all of this. But I have no idea why he's kidnapped Olivia. I know we don't know for sure that he has. But it's the only thing that makes sense to me. It could just be that he ran into her somewhere on Saturday. Olivia would have stopped to talk to him, because she knew she needed the info on a date for their final nomination meeting. She probably thought it would be a quick way to finish off another story. Just get the date and write it up."

Arni replied, "If he is as paranoid and obsessive as you think, maybe any approach by a reporter would have set him off. He's desperate. He wonders if she knows what he's done, and her original question is just a ruse to get him to incriminate himself."

"Yes, and then Olivia becomes just another loose end to tidy up." I shivered. What a horrifying thought.

"It would be great if Tyler Aston has recovered enough to talk to us. Let me get someone to go over to the hospital right away. If Tyler could give us any clue about who he suspected and where he went, not to mention who hit him over the head, we would be closer to having the grounds to search Jasper's house and property."

"But won't that take too long? What about Olivia? Can't you go back to Jasper's place now?"

"Zora, we're going to move on this. I think you've given me good information, but we have to do things right. It won't take long. It's just checking one last thing before potentially making a big mistake. That wouldn't help Olivia either."

After he hung up, I rushed out to ask Barbara if she'd been able to contact Brady. She shook her head with a worried look on her face. "Do you think you should have mentioned this to Arni? Both reporters missing?"

"Honestly, I'm not sure. I didn't want to divert his focus from Olivia, and I have a suspicion about what Brady might be up to."

"Playing detective?" she asked with a smile. "I think Brady has a crush on Olivia. I'm pretty sure he would be trying to do something to help."

"I don't know about the crush part. But I agree with you that he's out there trying to find her. I'm just worried that a man like Jasper who had one type of gun has other weapons. I don't want Brady to end up in the hospital."

"Or worse."

"Right."

I asked Barbara for the old paper phonebook and she dragged it out of the bottom drawer. Looking up Jasper Butler, I saw that he lived on a street called Muskrat Drive. I frowned. I'd never been there before as far as I could recall, but somehow it sounded familiar.

I got out my phone and put in the address. "That makes sense," I murmured. Muskrat was a small lane that led off Maple Hill Road. I had passed it on my way to Bernie's the other afternoon. It also made sense that the two brothers would live sort of near each other. And it would have made it extremely convenient for Jasper to nip out around the corner to Bernie's garage and dispose of Tyler in the trunk of Bertha.

I shook my head. What a despicable thing to do to his own brother. The man obviously had no conscience. Which did not bode well for one or more of my reporters. "I'm going out there," I told Barbara. "I won't go up to the house. Maybe just park nearby, or maybe drive past and see if I see anything. I don't know. That sounds ridiculous. But I'm going anyway. At least maybe I can track down Brady. I know I shouldn't even ask, but did either of them upload any stories before this crisis?"

"Yes. It looks like nearly everything was in. Olivia even sent the pictures from Saturday morning. I'm busy setting up a bunch of ads and working on the page layouts."

"Excellent. Listen, did you or any of your friends go to the Beer Festival?"

"We didn't, but my sister and a lot of my friends did."

"Great. Can you get in touch with them and get them to send

you a variety of photos? Then pick a couple that are clear and show either a panorama of the crowd, or even an attractive closeup of people enjoying themselves. We should be in pretty good shape for this week. I'll send you a brief story about my chat with Cowboy Whitmore. A little later."

31

I sat in the car and took another look at the map on my phone. I was responsible enough to know that, as much as I wanted to find both Brady and Olivia, I didn't want to mess up any police operation that Arni might be planning.

Nevertheless, I sure thought he was wasting his time. Jasper had invited the last officer who had visited him into his house. I didn't see why Arni couldn't just go out there and sit in the man's kitchen until he heard back from the hospital. Instead of leaving Jasper even more time and privacy to harm Olivia.

I knew there was nothing I could do to speed up his process. But I could look for Brady. And I was pretty sure I knew where he was.

The map showed Maple Hill Drive as a main road running west out of town, and Muskrat Drive cutting off to the south as a smaller street. I expanded the map to zoom in and saw another route marked. It looked like a narrow seasonal road connected the two streets in a lazy arc a couple of miles past Bernie's house. I was leery about using it, but it could be my best option to avoid being seen driving by Jasper's place. Or interfering with Arni, who would for sure be driving there directly from where Muskrat intersected with Maple Hill.

Seasonal roads were a toss of the dice. Some were nice narrow gravel lanes, or even two sandy ruts with grass growing up the middle. Either of those options would be fine. My RAV would roll right along. But if there were deep washouts or channels, or too much exposed rock, I'd probably chicken out. Otherwise, they'd have to send a search party for me next.

Well, all I could do was give it a try. If the summer road turned out to be impassible I'd just reverse back out to Maple Hill and make a new plan.

I felt less jittery once I got the vehicle in motion. I had a purpose. Find Brady and see what he knew. I didn't let my mind explore the options for rescuing Olivia. Brady was a good guy but he was no Bruce Willis.

I cruised north out of town, turned onto Maple Hill Road, and drove at a sensible pace out past Bernie's. Then I slowed even further, looking for the turn onto the summer road. With all the burgeoning foliage on the trees, bushes looking like they were on steroids, and the ditches full of reeds and wild irises, it was easy for me to miss the path. But at least I noticed it on the way by. I backed up and turned in.

This section of the road was fine. Yes, it was narrow, and alders and other plants scratched on the RAV's sides and doors, but it was in good shape so far. I made my way a good two or three miles before I ran into trouble. And not for any of the reasons I had expected. Brady drove an old silver Civic and there it was, parked in front of me, blocking my route. I was surprised he got it this far.

I got out and walked around the front of his car to have a look. Good for him. He'd had the sense to not carry on through a mini-lake. The road had descended gradually as it headed south on the way to hook up with Muskrat Drive and now led through a marshy area. Standing water covered the entire road. The RAV would have been fine, but Brady's car didn't have the clearance to pass through safely.

I sighed and looked at my feet. I was going to have to sacrifice these boots. I was wearing one of my new outfits. It was a hot summer day, and the bugs were already circling down here in Mosquito Central. I had on a long-sleeved tunic with wide bright pink and white stripes. I was very happy about the coverage but, even so, I doubted I'd escape unbitten. I was also wearing khaki jeggings and pale pink lace-up boots. They looked like Docs but thank goodness they were not. So sad to think that their next trip would likely be to the landfill.

Now that I knew I was on the right track, no pun intended, I locked the RAV, slung my bag crossways over my body and stepped smartly through the water. I don't know which I was more afraid of: leeches crawling inside my boots, snakes lurking in the bulrushes, or snapping turtles ready to turn on me. Or Jasper. Or muskrats, for that matter.

After five minutes, I was out of the hazard-filled water and climbing. I was soon a bit out of breath. The sun blazed down, Muskrat Road seemed to be in the distance at the top of a steep hill, and mosquitos were trying to feast on my ears. At least the map seemed to have been correct. This summer road had clearly been used during the past cottage season, and probably by snowmobilers as well. I was sure it was going to lead to my destination.

It felt like forever, but it was probably just another 15 minutes until I saw Muskrat Road ahead of me. I stayed well out of sight and fished out my phone. Was there a signal? Yes, indeed. I tried Brady again, but no luck. I guessed that he must have his device switched off for his top-secret mission. I shouldn't make fun of him, I thought. Not a bad idea. I switched mine off as well.

Since I didn't have any idea where Jasper lived, and there were no dwellings in sight, I walked out onto the road and headed left as quickly as I could, scanning the woods on either side of me. The surrounding forest ranged from airy pine plantations to a dense mix of spruce, poplar, raspberry canes, and wildflowers. I saw no signs of Brady. But I certainly didn't want to take a chance by calling his name.

Suddenly a small rock landed in front of me. I knew squirrels were, thankfully, not that smart or aggressive. I stood still and looked around. Brady's head popped up from a thicket of beech saplings. I glanced up and down the road, saw no one, and stepped into the woods. He put his finger to his lips and pointed further down the road. I figured that meant Jasper's house was nearby, but I was more concerned with the fact that Olivia was lying unconscious at his feet.

A million questions ran through my mind, but I knew I had to keep quiet and think. I whispered, "You found her! Where?"

"In a shed at Jasper's. I actually knew where she was before the sun came up but the door was locked. I had to wait for him to start making some noise before I could break in. Eventually, he turned on a radio on the front porch and started detailing his car."

"How did you get in?"

"There was a woodpile and a stump for splitting. And an ax."

"Fantastic. What's your plan?"

"No plan. I just wanted to get her out of there."

"Well, top marks for that. I've been so worried about her. How has she been? Unconscious the whole time? This doesn't look good."

"No. She's been drifting in and out. I was trying to keep her awake for a little while. But then she was in a lot of pain and the light was too bright. Once I ducked in here behind these beeches, she sort of fell back to sleep."

"Well, I hope it's sleep and not a coma," I said. "Sorry," I added when I saw the discouraged look on his face.

"I hope so too," he muttered. "So, what do you think?"

"Well, we can do one of two things. If we can carry her back down the seasonal road, my vehicle is parked behind yours. Or we can take a chance and wait where we are. I think the police will be out here soon."

I glanced down at poor Olivia. Brady had placed her on her side and propped her head and shoulders up on his backpack, but she wasn't moving.

"Has she said anything?"

"No. It seems the same as with Tyler. I guess she turned her back on him and he hit her with something. All I know is, she's alive."

Brady was looking a little pale himself underneath the smeared mud and scratches that marked his face. Up all night, hiking, hiding, breaking in, carrying Olivia. It had taken its toll.

I said, "I think we should wait here. I'm going to turn my phone back on and text Arni."

I heard what sounded like an ATV start up, and we exchanged glances. Brady said, "That's what I was afraid of. But I think we'll be ok if we can move further back away from the road. There's no way he can see us."

He looked at my shirt. It sure was bright. "OK, you're right. I'm going. I'll head straight back and lie on the ground. I'm pretty sure you'll be safe right here." I couldn't believe I'd said I would lie on the ground. If any muskrats came near me, I had no idea what I might do. Why couldn't this road be called Daisy Lane or something?

I pushed my way through the woods for another 50 feet or so and kept my word, tucking myself down among some low black-berry bushes. On the bright side, they had no fruit, so I didn't have to worry about bears sniffing me out.

32

I leaned up on my elbows, got out my phone, and turned it on. My text to Arni was succinct, *'We have Olivia, catch Jasper, call ambulance.'*

All of a sudden it was like real life was providing a sound-track to my text. The ATV had been putt-putting along at first. I assumed the driver was Jasper, moving slowly, scanning the woods for Olivia, just like a hunter tracking deer in early November.

But now the ATV driver gunned it. It roared steadily close to us. The good news was I could hear more engines approaching as well and, behind them in the distance, sirens.

I thought for sure Jasper had other things on his mind at this point, so I decided to take a chance and go back up closer to the road with Brady and Olivia. I walked along in a kind of fake crouch. I didn't want to put my knee out or strain my back, but I wanted to hide. More or less. I soon reached them and collapsed beside Olivia.

Brady finally looked happy. Still worried of course, but I could tell he was relieved. Seeing as I still had my phone in my hand, I took a few quick photos of the two of them. "Sorry," I whispered.

"I know," he replied. "Deadline tomorrow."

All the vehicles were almost in front of us now. Brady elbowed me and over the racket and said, "Video. Turn the phone sideways."

I snapped to it, stood up, and caught the action of Jasper whizzing by on the four-wheeler, followed by two police vehicles, first a Chevy Tahoe and then a sedan.

Sitting back down, I said to Brady, "That'll look great on the website." I was just trying to cheer him up. I think he knew it.

A second or two later, I heard the ATV take the right turn down the seasonal road I had just climbed up. Feeling safe now, I heaved a deep breath and stood up again, heading out to the road to see if the ambulance was in sight. This crimefighting was exhausting.

Unfortunately, the ambulance was not in view. I decided the fastest way to locate it without trotting all over the highlands outside Williamsport was to call the 911 operator. I said, "I'm calling from Muskrat Drive. Do you have an ambulance out here?" When the operator said yes, I explained, "The victim has a serious head injury and is located a short distance from where your paramedics are parked. Can you ask them to drive in half a mile further?"

Seconds later, I saw the flashing lights and waved my arms at them from the middle of the road.

Now it was me who was relieved. The paramedics handled Olivia with the utmost care and were soon whisking her off to the hospital.

Brady looked towards the corner and seemed to be himself again. I knew we should follow the action, but I said, "One second." I dialed Richard Park. "Good news. We found her. She has a head injury, and the ambulance is on the way to the hospital. But she's alive. Yes. See you there later today."

Brady and I ended up having a ringside view. It was almost like sitting in an amphitheater except it was real life, not a play. We reached the corner. The police department sedan was parked there but was empty so we carried on down the road. It sure was easier walking in this direction. Also, as the road straightened it gave us a bird's eye view. We just stopped and watched.

I knew we were likely too far away for the video camera on my phone, but I ran it anyway. I saw Brady look over to make sure I was holding it horizontally. "Don't worry," I said. "I remembered." That actually got a short laugh from him.

In the distance, we saw the ATV zooming down the narrow lane. The police SUV had almost caught up and was basically just following. I thought if Jasper made it through the water, our parked cars would help the police. He would have to steer around them and the thick underbrush would definitely slow him down.

But it never came to that. Jasper was going way too fast for the transition between gravel and water, and as soon as he hit the marshy section, the front wheels of the ATV stopped short and Jasper went flying. If we ever decided to use the video, we'd have to strip the sound out of it. Because the whole thing just struck both Brady and me as hilarious and we were screaming with laughter.

After a few minutes, we regained our composure and strolled closer. Brady got some good shots of the officers dragging Jasper out of the swamp. He seemed unharmed, just sopping wet. I hoped the leeches had found him.

We found a little clearing where we could stand to get out of the way as the officers backed their SUV up the track to Muskrat

Road. I smiled and waved at Arni as he drove by, and he gave me a discreet 'thumbs up.'

At this point, Brady and I could return to our cars. "You may as well give me a head start. I hate backing up and it's going to take me forever."

He nodded, and said, "It's OK. I really want to get to the hospital, but I know they won't have any information yet."

I backed the RAV out of the summer road without any problems and while I waited for Brady, I called both Barbara and Marley with the good news about Olivia and Jasper. I indulged myself and also phoned Darius.

I then started dictating an account of what we'd all been through in the last 48 hours, from Olivia's disappearance to Jasper's capture. By this time tomorrow, the paper had to be ready to go to the printers and it was going to be a close call this time. I listed a few topics for shorter stories related to the main one that I would write...

Fred and the Liberals. I dictated some notes about my conversation with Marley and Marion.

Jasper's arrest. We'd have Brady's picture and likely a still photo from the video I'd taken. Then we'd get the wording of the charges that would soon be laid by police and include that.

Brady's rescue of Olivia. He could write this up himself. That should more or less look after the front page plus one more.

In addition, there was the update on our mayoral candidates. Leona Rigg. I'd try to find Olivia's notes from her chat with Sonny or call him again myself. And I had my own details about Cowboy Whitmore.

It was going to be a long night, but I was pretty sure we'd have a compelling series of news stories for Whistle readers this week. I thought about ordering extra copies.

33

A s I expected, Tuesday had been an absolute madhouse. I'd probably end up slipping Barbara a little bonus, as I don't think we would have had a Williamsport Whistle on the streets today without her wide range of skills. We were a little late sending the paper to the printer, but she had worked several extra hours making sure it all came together.

I wasn't a huge fan of Second World War music, but I'd grown fond of Vera Lynn in the past day or so as she serenaded us via Barbara's desktop speakers. Very motivational.

Now, here we were on the second Wednesday in a row with the Whistle devoted mainly to the death of Mayor Fred Phipps and its aftermath. The town was abuzz with people buying and reading the paper. Many folks stopped into the office to visit and offer up comments, gossip, and tips for follow-up. All in all, it was a great day.

Even more so because both Tyler and Olivia were out of the hospital. And Brady was as cheery and hardworking as ever. His focus seemed to clear at the approximate time that Olivia got sent home.

I decided to order some pizzas and salad and while I was waiting for them to be delivered, I set up the back patio for a little picnic. Again, the sun was shining, and Rocco frisked around tossing his orange ball back and forth by himself because I told him I was too busy to play. I brushed off the picnic table and arranged some lawn chairs. Looking around in satisfaction, I saw that my grass was almost back to normal, and vowed to make a container garden this year.

By the time the pizzas arrived, I had set out some plastic plates and cutlery, glasses, and a pitcher of water, along with iced tea of course. As I was out front paying the delivery guy, I saw the Park family approaching. Olivia looked stylish as always. She was wearing a ball cap with a long beak, and large fashionable sunglasses. I waved at them, beckoning them in for lunch. Then I told Barbara to put up the 'Closed' sign and join us out back.

We all settled down and were diving into the meal when there was a tapping at the back gate. I went over, saw that it was Arni, and let him in. "There's plenty," I said. "Pull up a chair."

Then I raised a glass of iced tea and said, "Cheers. To our intrepid reporters. And in the future will you try to remember what they taught you in journalism school. You don't make the news, you just report it."

Everyone laughed and that seemed to loosen up the atmosphere. Then there was total silence for a while as people devoured pizza and salad. Which was fine with me. I was keeping pace with the rest of them, although I'd have to say Brady was the champ.

I turned to Arni and said, "You probably feel like you've walked into the lion's den, but you must have expected this. Can you give us an update?"

He laughed and said, "Sure. But there's not much more than you already know from the media releases. And your own paper.

Jasper Butler's being held without bail. We almost had to arrest Bernie, he was so mad at Jasper for trying to frame him. The best news of course is that Olivia and Tyler both seem to be recovering fine." Liz Park put her arm around Olivia's shoulders and gave her a squeeze.

"I appreciate that you think we did a good job, but I still have quite a few questions. For one, was Tyler on the right track? Did he suspect Jasper? And if so, why? That's the question that has been keeping us all up at night for nearly two weeks."

"Definitely," said Arni. "It was a combination of things. That night at the Legion, he noticed that Jasper kept taking his suit jacket on and off. Tyler wondered if it was because the gun was in the pocket. Secondly, Jasper was seated on the side of the hall nearest the bathrooms. And Jordan mentioned to him that Jasper had called on her dad at home, and that Fred had seemed annoyed afterward. Tyler put those things together and sort of guessed. He had no idea about the political stuff. He was just observant and decided to run his theory by Jasper. Instead of me. Unfortunately, he found out the hard way that he was correct."

I asked, "So were we right about the timing? Did Jasper move Tyler in the mid-afternoon?"

"Yup. Jasper's not saying much, but once we could talk to Tyler himself, the timeframe became clear."

I turned to Olivia, "If you'd rather not talk about it, I under-stand. But we've been so worried about you. And also, I feel guilty that I might have sent you into danger."

Olivia smiled and said, "No, it wasn't you. And I certainly never figured out any of the stuff that Tyler did. I was down taking pictures at the Craft Beer Festival. I saw Jasper and never thought anything of it. I knew I needed a quick word with him to find out when the Conservatives were going to finish up their nomination process."

I felt a wave of relief. Olivia had not been playing detective. And she had approached the man with a very simple query. Without knowing that he was insane and on a spree of killing and mayhem.

Arni said, "It seems exactly as you suspected, Zora. Nothing Olivia could have said or done would have made a difference. I think if any of the three of you had even looked sideways at him, he would have reacted the same way."

Olivia looked down and murmured. "I disagree. I should never have gotten in his car. But he said that it was so noisy and crowded at the Festival, and that he could refer to his notes. It's just," she hesitated. "He's an older man, and I thought he was nice and that I could trust him."

By now tears were rolling down her face. "It was like..."

I interrupted her. I figured her tears were not for herself and what she had endured being kidnapped and held prisoner by Jasper Butler, but because of her grief at the loss of Fred. At the same time, if she wanted to confess to her parents and the rest of the world, she should probably do that when she wasn't tired and concussed.

"Oh, Olivia, I'm sure we can all identify with that. It's not your fault at all. I think I've watched enough TV to know old Jasper doesn't fit the profile of a murderer."

Brady said, "I'm not sure about that. What about when they always say, 'He was quiet, lived alone and kept to himself.' Or, 'He was the nicest person, I just can't believe it.'"

At this, we all laughed, and I think Olivia looked relieved. I heard another knock at the gate to the laneway. I got up and opened it. Everyone was really happy to see Marley, especially as she was carrying a large strawberry rhubarb pie and a container of ice cream.

"Dessert!" said Brady.

Rocco stood up and clawed her knees until I ordered him to stop.

Once we were all stuffed full of pie and ice cream there was a lull of contentment. I leaned back in my chair and looked up at the sky. I was so thankful that the uncertainty and, well, fear of the past two weeks was now over.

Into the silence, Olivia spoke up. "So, Zora, I have a question. I know you're really busy, but I wondered if you might have time to go for a drive with me?"

At that point, I would have done just about anything for that young lady. "Yes, of course, Olivia. Any time."

"It's just that I have a couple of concert tickets, and I'm not ready to drive all the way to Toronto."

Brady couldn't contain himself and burst out laughing. He must have been in on it. I thought my heart would stop. "Not. Not to see Drake?" I whispered. "Oh. My. Gosh."

By then all the others were laughing too. But I felt tears forming in my eyes. It must have been all the drama of the past week. The fire that had almost taken out part of the historic downtown, not to mention most of my clothes. The incredible panic I had hidden at the thought that Olivia might have been seriously harmed. The stress of worrying about how the investigation might affect my business. Not to mention how touched I was that Olivia would invite me instead of a friend.

I swiped my hand over my eyes and said, "I can't even believe you'd take me. Are you sure?"

"Positive! It will be fun," she replied.

Arni had to have the last word, channeling Drake, "You used to call me on my cell phone. But you can stop any time."

The End

DEAR READERS,

I hope you enjoyed Book 1 of the **"Poodle Versus..."** series!

To get the Free Prequels to all my series, please sign up for my newsletter. You'll also get updates on books and me, and, of course, some cute dog pictures. Newsletter Signup.

As a new author, it would mean so much to me if you could page forward and leave a review of *Poodle Versus The Assassin*. Thank you!

And, feel free to take a sneak peek at *Poodle Versus The Mob*, on the next page!

POODLE VERSUS THE MOB

Stop the presses! Rocco's digging up the evidence.

Chapter 1

t was just after 5:30 in the morning and Rocco and I were out exploring. Some might call it snooping. Sneaking around.

Or, if you want to get picky, trespassing.

My pet dog Rocco was a very special breed - NSP, or Nasty Small Poodle. His curly beige fur and bright black eyes gave him a friendly, happy-go-lucky air. But this hid the soul of a medieval prince, ruthless ruler of all he surveyed.

At the moment, he was following his nose. I got such a laugh when I saw the social media meme about dogs 'checking their pee-mail.' Rocco was a constant correspondent, receiving and of course sending numerous messages, several times a day.

Even though it was summer, the sun was not yet up. The eastern sky had a pale pink glow and the lights along Main Street were bright enough to illuminate our way. Rocco and I were both fascinated by the new construction project on the corner, a block from my apartment.

Our daily visit to the work site filled me with anticipation.

For years I had been a Main Street resident. I owned a narrow historic property that had two separate storefronts. One was used by my business. The Williamsport Whistle was our hometown newspaper. Despite the odds, it was still managing to thrive even in the era of online media.

Beside us was a fabulous café, Coyote Coffee. I was looking forward to my latte fix when I returned from my morning walk. Occupying the space above both stores was my current apartment. It was unique and quaint, and I wasn't really searching for anywhere else to live. I'd been happy there for so long, and it truly was home sweet home.

But when the King William Mews condos went up for sale, I was hooked. The location was perfect. It would be just a short walk to the office. I'd still have my downtown home base. And I was totally in love with the floor plan of my new penthouse home. Yes, that's right, penthouse. So what if the local height restrictions meant I'd be looking over the town from the fifth floor? I would be up above the other roofs and looking down on the treetops.

I imagined that the condo would have a very different ambiance when compared to my little apartment. Spacious instead of cozy, open and filled with light, not a series of small rooms laid out shotgun-fashion. I would still have a large balcony and I was pretty sure Prince Rocco would adapt to the elevator.

By the time we had circled the block and arrived to check out the progress on the condos, it was a little brighter. I got out my phone to take a photo. I wasn't being very scientific about it, but I still took a picture a day to show how the construction was coming along.

Unfortunately, while I was fiddling with the phone, I dropped Rocco's leash. Before I could bend down and pick it up, he was gone.

In a flash he was under the chain-link gate, sprinting across the dusty gravel yard and ducking into the shadowy interior of the building. I was a little worried. I could only imagine the dangers that might lie in the path of an insane poodle, darting around a dark construction site. Not to mention he had always been the kind of dog that would eat anything. It was a wonder he had survived to his present age of 11.

I grabbed the gate and gave it a good shake. Locked. As I expected. I sighed. I had to get the dog back, and he sure wasn't responding to my shouts, of "Rocco, come!"

I tried yelling, "Leave it!" for good measure. That might make him drop anything toxic out of his mouth and come running to me for a treat. But not this time. There was no sign of him.

I walked slowly around the perimeter of the fence. After a moment I saw I was in luck. Where the safety fence met the adjacent building there was a bit of a gap.

I looked at it critically. I was in pretty good shape for my age, which had crept over the 50-year mark a while ago. I probably had the poodle, wherever he was, to thank for that. With our regular hikes around town, and my height of 5'8" to spread a few extra pounds over, I usually felt good about my appearance. However, the longer I looked at that gap the narrower it seemed.

I turned sideways, sucked in my stomach, and tried to squeeze through. The first few inches went fine.

But then I heard the ominous ripping noise of cotton tearing. I had two choices. Keep sliding between the wall and the fence and see what exactly was torn once I was inside. Or stop.

Stopping didn't seem like a good choice. I felt like I was in a prison yard, with my nose against the brick wall. No thank you.

I wormed my way past the fence and took stock of my clothing. It was not a pretty sight. It looked like a piece of the wire fencing had caught in the pocket of my capris. My behind was now air-conditioned with a huge triangular tear across the back of the pants. On top of that, I discovered I was wearing novelty panties with big red hearts and cartoon donkey heads. The slogan was sort of unnecessary, but it said, "Kiss My" over and over. Between the hearts. OK, I admit it, I got dressed in the dark.

Grabbing the cotton cloth, I tried to hold my pants together as I picked my way carefully across the rough patch in front of the building. It was crisscrossed with deep ruts from all the truck traffic and I didn't want to trip over my own two feet.

It would be so embarrassing if I hurt myself in a fall. I'd be trapped inside a prohibited work site, lying there with my donkeys hanging out, waiting to be rescued by the first workers to arrive. I shuddered. I was too old for this nonsense. Literally.

Not to mention, I was already breaking a number of laws. There had been a lot of signs hanging on the outside of that chain-link fence. 'No Admittance,' of course. Not to mention 'Hard Hats and Safety Boots must Be Worn At All Times.' I didn't think that a baggy white t-shirt, ripped magenta cotton capris and running shoes qualified. And I also didn't believe that my Toronto Blue Jays ball cap would do much to protect my skull if anything fell on it.

When I got to the front wall of the building I felt I had no choice but to enter. That wasn't much of a problem, as there were no windows or doors yet. At the moment, the King William Mews was mostly a skeleton structure. A pattern of iron posts, beams, and girders extended into the dim interior.

Dog or no dog, I was fascinated. I could imagine a floor plan for the shops and restaurants that would be occupying the expansive main floor someday soon. That would be the Mews, no doubt. Above, would rise four floors of apartments for all us lucky condo buyers.

The sun had risen further in the sky and there was now a

fair bit of light shining in from the openings that would be future picture windows. I could see that the building site was a busy one. Tools and equipment had been left in place, ready for the new day's work. Rakes, shovels, buckets, and trowels were set neatly along one wall, in a large open space.

From what I could see, it seemed as though this stage of the project involved pouring the concrete floors. Most of the main level was finished, forming a smooth, cool, gray surface. I walked a little faster, calling for Rocco.

Further in towards the core of the building, some interior walls had already been erected. Utility rooms, I figured, plus the elevator shaft. I sighed. Where was that crazy animal? I wanted to find him and escape from this place before I got caught.

That was all I needed. There was something deliciously ironic and entertaining to the local citizens of Williamsport when they could catch the publisher of their local paper doing something silly or undignified. I'd never live it down if I got charged with breaking into what I already considered to be my own home. Not to mention the state of my wardrobe.

I could hear a weird noise from my left so I jogged over to one small room and glanced inside. Finally. "Rocco, come here, right now," I scolded him.

"*You must be joking,*" I was sure I heard him retort. Did my dog really talk? I wasn't sure. But it wasn't hard to imagine his response in any given situation. If any dog could communicate with a glance, a gesture, a pose, a raised eyebrow, or a curl of the lip, it was my Rocco. His dialogue and snide commentary were the next natural step.

"No, I'm not joking. We have to get out of here. Nasty boy. Stop that."

He looked like he was frantically trying to dig a hole to China. His front feet were flashing so fast they were a blur. I had to say he wasn't making much headway in the concrete.

"Come on, stop it. You're going to set your paws on fire." I was surprised the friction on his feet hadn't stopped him by now. They must have been heating up.

It was fairly dark in the room, which wasn't much bigger than a walk-in closet, and I was blocking the little available light with my own shadow. I stepped inside to try and get a better look. There was a two-by-six board across the doorway creating the front edge of a step, making the interior floor a bit higher than the rest of the room.

I changed position again to let more light in. Weird. This portion of floor seemed rougher than the rest of the building. Out in the main part of the Mews, the floor surface was as smooth as ice, no pits or flaws. But the closet floor seemed more textured. A bit gravelly. Rocco was still determined to dig a hole in it. He wouldn't need his nails trimmed for quite a while after this workout.

The more I looked at the floor in the little room, the odder it appeared. I was getting a bad feeling about this. At one end of the room, there were a couple of concrete-covered bumps. And at the other end, where Roc was trying to dig, it almost looked like it was breaking up a bit.

"Hey, you stay here," I said unnecessarily. I left the closet and went back to where I had seen the shovels. Hoisting one over my shoulder, I returned and entered the room. Rocco was still ignoring me so I returned the favor. I headed over to the bumpy area and tried to chip away around them. To my surprise, the concrete was breaking up easily.

I frowned. This didn't seem like very good quality control on the site of my future home. I thought I was buying into a high-end project. The price tag certainly said that. And yet here I was, a fifty-ish woman, hacking it to pieces with a borrowed shovel.

I jabbed at the floor some more, and hunks of concrete flew up and landed to one side. Suddenly, Rocco darted past me to the area where I had been chipping away. He started digging furiously in that spot. I took the shovel and gently scraped away what I could.

I squinted in the gloom. No way. It couldn't be. Faster than you could say Jimmy Hoffa, I deduced that we had just unburied two leather-shoe-clad feet.

I wanted to get out onto the sidewalk before calling the police. I thought it would look better to say I had chased the dog inside, rather than calling from the scene of the crime. So to speak.

But I never forgot my calling as a journalist. The flash was blinding as I took a series of quick photos.

Read the rest of the book now! Click here.

"POODLE VERSUS..." SERIES

A 50-something local newspaper publisher and a pampered prince of a poodle stumble upon a number of shocking crimes in a cottage-country small town.

It's up to Zora Flynn and her nasty small poodle Rocco to sort out a distinctive cast of characters in the town of Williamsport and find the murderer.

Meet Zora. She's one of a kind, flavored with a dash of Agatha Raisin and a splash of Stephanie Plum, and her exploits and foibles will have you laughing out loud.

Her small dog, Rocco, wears a bright blue collar studded with yellow crowns. With his regal personality, he amuses Zora with his snide comments and princely demands. Despite this, he is a poodle of action. And Zora's secret weapon.

Surrounded by rocky cliffs, pristine lakes, and picture-perfect scenery, Williamsport is a charming town in cottage country. But mysterious crimes often cast a shadow in the friendly waterfront community.

It probably goes without saying, but the **Poodle Versus...** series is good, clean fun, except for the occasional suspicious death. No graphic violence, sex or swearing.

Poodle Versus The Assassin is the highly entertaining first book in an ongoing cozy mystery series starring Zora and Rocco.

I think you'll also enjoy the rest of the books!

Poodle Versus The Mob Pre-order July 1, launch August 1

Poodle Versus The Killer Pre-order August 1, launch September 1

Poodle Versus The Yeti Pre-order September 1, launch October 1

Poodle Versus The Butcher Pre-order October 1, launch November 1

Poodle Versus The Fake Santa Pre-order November 1, launch December 1

And more in 2021!

MURDER IN SEASON SERIES

Don't miss out! This fast-paced cozy mystery trilogy has lots of action but no graphic violence, sex or swearing.

Book 1, Frozen Fear

There's been a suspicious death in this sleepy, snowy town, and I'm facing a blizzard of clues and suspects.

I really didn't need one more problem.

First, I got shot in the line of duty. Then everyone blamed me, Detective Constable Claire Beckett, for my boss getting killed. Believe it or not, all I want is to clear my name and get my job back.

I retreated up north to my family's quaint log cottage so my shoulder could heal, and my friend Sid lent me his dog Kojak. Kojak and I both love lying on the couch. He takes time out to chase squirrels, and I obsess over my upcoming disciplinary hearing.

Meanwhile, a woman who just happens to look like my twin has been killed. Seriously. Wouldn't that make you stop and think? Or act like a cop, and investigate?

Book 2, *Holiday Homicide*

I was all about the sun, sand, and surf. But I had to think twice about this winter holiday once we had a slaying. Talk about trouble in paradise!

My childhood friend, travel writer Serena St. James, invited me, Detective Constable Claire Becket, to join her on this amazing gig. I wasn't doing much at home, other than recovering from being shot and panicking over my disciplinary hearing.

Serena and I love this luxury resort, but apparently we're rubbing shoulders with a killer.

The local police chief has actually asked me for help in sorting out the suspects. Maybe I'm getting my mojo back. If I can stay alive long enough to enjoy it.

Book 3, *Twister Terror*

The tornado was bad enough. Can we agree on that?

There's more. I've also managed to witness a hit-and-run, my garage was set on fire and they finally told me a date for my disciplinary hearing.

I may not be Detective Constable Claire Beckett for much longer. Help! My job means everything to me.

Mind you I've had a bit of assistance. I'm still dog-sitting Kojak, and he chased down a clue. And my neighbor Miles Gallagher has warmed up to me, and the dog. Miles is in town, and I asked him to bring his superhero cape. And wear it.

I just need one final piece to the puzzle. And I don't care what it takes. I'll find it.

Newsletter and Free Prequels

I'd like to invite you to sign up for my Newsletter. You'll get the Free Prequels to all my series, updates on books and me, and of course, cute dog photos. Newsletter Signup.

ABOUT ANNE SHILLOLO

What can I tell you?

They say 'write what you know,' and most days I feel like I'm being held hostage by the original NSP - nasty small poodle.

My real-life Rocco is 15 pounds of non-stop energy and vengeful behavior. He's the inspiration for the character of the same name in my books. Roc is actually trying to claim a writing credit, since so many of his shenanigans have ended up on the page.

I believe I hear him now. If he could really talk, he'd be saying, *"Great Merciful Poodles, can't you write faster? It's time for my hourly game of Fetch."*

I love writing every day and the result so far is two cozy mystery series, and counting. Murder In Season features injured detective constable Claire Beckett. That trilogy is followed by the Poodle Versus... series. Starring - guess who?

So far, I've left out my husband, and our little house in the woods. But who knows? Maybe in the next series...

To get the Free Prequels to all my series, please sign up for my newsletter. You'll also get updates on books, me, and The Rockinator. Newsletter Signup.

You can find me on Facebook as Anne Shillolo Writer, and I'm a longtime Twitter user @anneshillolo. As you might imagine, my website is AnneShillolo.com.

Made in the USA
Monee, IL
01 September 2020

40371954R00114